# GHOST

# HOUSE

# GHOST HOUSE

## R.M. Kinder

HENDERSON, NEVADA

Copyright 2024 by R. M. Kinder

Cover Design by Kristine Lowe-Martin
Formatting by Stephanie Flint

All rights reserved. Published by LiquidAmber Publishing.

**Ebook ISBN: 978-0-9895034-8-8**
**Paperback ISBN: 978-0-9895034-7-1**

**LiquidAmber Publishing**
**Henderson, Nevada**

# Contents

*Mercy Baldwin heard a knocking, knocking,*

*heard it calling at the window,*

*the wind oh, the wind oh.*

*Mercy Baldwin heard a knocking,*

*ran she quick the windows locking,*

*for she knew who was a-knocking,*

*at her blind girl's window.*

*Not the wind, no, not the wind, no.*

# PART I

# EARLY JANUARY

## ANNA

**In this house,** the air goes quiet, sometimes for years. There are many rooms, more than the eyes see, a little nook here sealed, a short door in a shadowed corner, with a whisper-quiet latch, a window that shouldn't open, but does. Music plays through the house, like promises before they're broken, hopes before they're dashed. Outside, night breezes beckon one to have a breath of air, just a breath. The moon rides low, white and lonely. All the roads lead somewhere, but not everyone can travel. One can think and be, and turn and be, but not turn back and be. I dream where I have been.

My name is Anna. I waken sometimes to the sound of music, birds, wind, a voice, and perhaps from longing, which is also why I sleep. I'm slow to wake, unsure which time I'm in. I do try to care for this house as always—want to care for it, because it's my home, and dear to me—but I must learn again. I work at learning. I can see my son, speak with him, kiss his cheek, take his hand, and feel again that love I have for him. When he's not my son, but the other, as now, I'm wary. I look for a sign. He was fond of signs. I think they built a semblance of place for him, like living amid splinters when no abode is possible. Some people want to leave their mark on this earth with great efforts, others with kindness. He leaves pain. My boundaries are the walls of this house. I don't know his boundaries or his powers.

A young woman comes, tall, and fiery haired. She hugs her coat around her and brrrs her broad shoulders against the cold. She lights a small cigar and stands by the vehicle to study the house. She's a brazen thing. Endearing. If I could move as I did when alive, I would fly out to her. Run! Run! I would say. Don't look at him! Don't think on him! Run!

He has seen the visitor, surely, but it's me he watches now. She throws the cigar to the ground and approaches the house. She's at the side window, peering in. "Hallooo?" It's a warm voice.

I stay between him and the window. He doesn't move from the chair where he lounges, long-limbed, young, scornful. Not my son. I amuse him. I try to transmit my fear to her. Go!

She hurries to the fore of the house and from a room there I see her on the deep porch. She peers where I stand. Does she see me? She shields her eyes, stares at me, but turns away.

Then to her vehicle. She's inside it, leaving. I'm both pleased and sorry. It's good that she is safe. But I ache.

"There will be five of them," he says.

"You mustn't hurt any of them."

"Yes."

The answer that is no answer. He's gone. Ostensibly. Except for one place in this house, he watches what he wants when he wants.

If they are truly coming, I should write it all down, my memories, my thoughts, my understanding of what abides here. I could begin with the day I found the pipe in the basement, with its long metal cap lying beside it. I could smell the underground vastness, the scent of deep, old waters, a whisper of movement, subtle, unceasing. I wanted to replace the cap, but then I wondered what if something had come out, and was still out, and I prevented it from returning.

I fetched William, who was not at all concerned. "Maybe one of the girls did it," he said, meaning a hired girl or a student. "Or even a raccoon. They're crafty. They can get into anything."

"It's too heavy for a creature to lift."

He started to set the cap, but I asked him to leave it at least a while.

"Why call me then? I see. You think something came out and you want to drive it back in."

He knew me. We had talks about my fancies, things I had heard about, read about, conjectured. Entrances to the netherworld, where one might be dragged and imprisoned. Where souls flutter in despair. Where birds, flying above, die from the fumes.

"You know more than is good for you, Anna. That mind of yours churns up too many possibilities."

"I only listen," I told him. "I learn. I don't manufacture. Others come up with theories. I consider them, if they are probable, possible, or impossible."

"And do you consider anything impossible, my girl?"

More so then.

I go about the great room so my son's usurper can see that I'm mistress still, and I can feel that I am. I wear the clothing I died in, though I have choices. It's a dress I made myself, the color of larkspur, with pink sprigs over all but yoke and collar, and it skims the toe top of my shoes. The sleeves are long and straight, with deep cuffs. I fashioned the dress after a colored plate in a ladies' catalog. My William had said, "This would become you." So it did. I wear it for him, for me, for what was and wasn't and can't be again.

I've wondered if I loved my husband more than my son. No. I loved them both. I love them now.

# THE WOMEN

**Friday afternoon, 4:00 p.m.,** the women meet in a vacant parking lot to travel together in one vehicle. A cloudless gray sky broods overhead and the dropping temperature confirms the cold spell forecast. They aren't concerned about the weather, because rain, even an ice storm, suits the experience they crave, and the house is supposed to be comfortable and lovely, fitted as a rental by the county historical society. They're dressed for a drafty old residence. They have adequate food supplies. This is what they want to do. They're excited and happy. They leave the car radio off so nothing will impinge on the trip they're beginning.

Though they don't know each other well, they have belonged to the same book club for over a year and have realized they share common interests—the strange and unknown, particularly ghosts. Melody, seamstress; Rachel, aspiring writer; Deborah, high school literature teacher; Shelley, realtor's assistant; Connie, librarian assistant at Mason's small university.

Thirty miles from Mason, Rachel drives across a rattling plank bridge and onto a rutted, partially graveled upgrade. To the right a fenced, uneven field runs parallel to the highway; to the left leafless trees hold the rain-gullied slope. Up higher, in a sliver of twilight, the house looms. They ease into the dirt side yard and appraise the building from that limited angle: two-stories, maybe three, dark blue clapboard, two lower windows. Just beyond the house are hunched silhouettes of headstones.

The rear door is unlocked, as they had been advised, and they unload quickly into the boxy entry, a kind of mudroom. Rachel finds a key on the kitchen counter, with it a business card offering the image of a black-haired man clutching a fiddle and bow. On the back is his printed message: "All is in order. If you need anything, I'll come straightaway."

"That's Luke Essex," Melody says. "He does a lot of work for the historical society."

"Handsome guy."

"Yes."

They tour, anxious to enjoy slowly. They'll tell only two stories tonight, the others tomorrow night. Pockets of light downstairs and up suggest warmth and occupancy but the windows are curtainless. The whole place is decently furnished, some old wood pieces, some replicas, all lovely, polished, with deep wood grains. The bedrooms are small except for one, and have nice touches, steamer trunk or hat boxes, chair, wardrobe—something. A basket of colorful quilts is to one side of the landing.

When one woman turns sharply or takes a quick breath, the others pause. They do feel a ghost is present, not in a strong way, perhaps from their own wishful thinking. They're willing to linger and allow something to unfold. After a while, they more easily investigate a little distance apart.

Downstairs they discover stacks of old newspapers in a front room office, dating from the 1870s, but decide they're reproductions. A music room contains an ancient piano with cracked, yellow keys. Framed photos of young girls, each with a violin, decorate the walls. Maybe a conservatory? Sixteen students back then, in these backwoods, would have been impressive. Beautiful girls, every one of them.

# SUPPER

**As they eat** the small sandwiches, nuts, and tidbits of fruit that Melody prepared, they talk of kinds of ghosts, poltergeists who rain stones and frogs on roofs, break lamps, throw glasses, trip a person, jerk covers off. Shadow people who are often children and dart across paths and hallways. They're shy and somehow the most sad. "They're lonely," Melody says. "They want a mother." Apparitions who glide silently, transparent or full-bodied, who moan and weep. Web ghosts who reveal their presence by a spidery film one walks into without seeing and must wipe away. Spheres like huge water drops filled with an image or spirit. They wonder about ghosts' abilities. Can ghosts speak without a medium? Why do recordings of ghost voices always sound so bassy and slow, or wavery, as if under water? Why are ghosts' moans audible and not their words? How can ghosts transport solid items, like keys, without the item being seen? If ghosts' weight makes floors creak, why don't walls stop them? Any consistent rules at all?

"Maybe they have a transforming power that varies in degrees among them," Shelley says, fiddling with the base of her upturned wine glass—she has explained she doesn't drink liquor. "Or maybe they draw power from living individuals."

Seances, Ouija boards, ectoplasm, fakes. Mediums.

"True mediums don't advertise themselves," Shelley says. "They can die in a channeling. The exertion is so extreme their blood vessels may burst."

As they begin clearing the table, Connie says softly to Shelley, "Forgive me if this is invasive. Are you a medium? You know so much."

"No. And I wouldn't be if I could."

# ANNA

**It is apoplexy** Shelley described. I knew a priest who feared that risk. Shelley remains at the table, her head bowed into the shield of her hands, her blond curls thick enough to hide coins. She could be praying or crying. I rest my hands on her shoulders, to comfort. A shudder flows into me! She is afraid! Of me? I stand back. I see the women bustling around, their surreptitious looks at Shelley, who rises and begins to help them arrange the room.

I believe a poltergeist might be something other than a prankster, something undeveloped and perhaps trainable — most creatures are trainable. Or perhaps it is just the energy of anger and great desire taking form and acting. God knows. Perhaps his budding power was chaos. I won't believe that he himself is a prankster. I will think better of him than that. Perhaps that will help him be better than that. If he hears me, he may pardon my thoughts given where I am.

The women will tell stories about ghosts. I'm eager to know what they know. I follow them but stay by the breakfront, from where I may see both sides of the great room and thus know if he my son's captor joins us. The women make shadows against the floor and walls and each other. I look behind me and around my feet. Nothing. No shadow from me. If I could step from where I am into where they are, would I? If I could save both John and them, yes. I long to be with the living world again.

# FRIDAY,
# MIDEVENING
# RACHEL'S STORY

**Sitting sideways on** the raised stone hearth, Rachel draws deeply on a cigarette, tosses the butt into the fire and exhales so the smoke will float up the chimney. Deborah and Connie have turned off electric lights and brought kerosene lamps and candles into this part of the great room. They've positioned a davenport, settee, and chairs to face the double fireplace. Rachel can see the upstairs landing and the huge window there, a block of night, like a portal to another world. God's eye. A refrain from her childhood pops up: *Claws, nails, hammer, wood, keep me safe, keep me good.* That was her chant as night approached, to protect herself from God and the other, whatever it was. She shakes her head, smiles toward her friends. She recalls for herself the encounter she's sharing with them.

It was a silvery night, August, moist and heavy. She drove with the window down and the air whipped cool around her. The two-lane road was empty, rural, all hers, the distant trees like scalloped shadows. Oh, she was happy — at first. The huge moon hung near, so bright over the whole landscape that she turned off the headlights and drove in a kind of beautiful twilight. She saw something on the shoulder ahead and switched the lights on, caught this brown blur she thought was a dust devil or a swarm of insects, but it was a person turning toward her, face stark white just as she passed. She reasoned with herself that she hadn't seen a young man, only light into a dust cloud, or maybe even a bush, but she remembers he hadn't been alone. A low and round creature had been with him. Porcine. Maybe a dog. Whatever, they were both behind her. A few minutes later, she realized she needed to find a restroom. She was in the boondocks, no way to go but primitive, so she took the first road off that was open enough likely no creature could hide, raccoon, possum, wildcat. Killer. She left the motor running, the lights on low, and got out, surveying the situation. All was clear. On the hill was a long white house with dark windows, everyone asleep or gone. She had slipped around the car door to be modest from the highway. She was jumpy — the noise of peeing was so personal, so very loud out in the wilderness and she thought about how female scents drew fierce animals, even bears, though uncommon in this area. Some acts a person can't hurry. When she stood up, zipping her pants, she knew something was behind her. Close. She listened without turning, and sort of edged around the door slowly, daring a look only as she slid into the seat. The same guy! She slammed the door and got out of there. She was terrified all the way into Mason that he would be by the road again.

Rachel stops, stretches the neck of her sweater and hugs herself. "That's my story," she says. "If I'd only seen him once, I'd think I had mistaken a sign for a person. But to see him twice that many miles apart? It was a man, but he couldn't have traveled that far that fast. Could he have been a ghost? Does that kind of sighting fit?"

"I've been thinking about that house you saw on top of the hill," Melody says. "There was a murder in that area, a real brutal one, when I was in grade school. A gang of boys had hurt a girl. She was about fifteen. They used her, but that wasn't enough for them. You may have been on the same property, Rachel. About fifteen miles north of Clinton? You could have intercepted a haunting."

"You said it was a girl who died. I saw a man."

"Another possibility," Connie says, "is that you caught the *mindset* of someone. You caught a memory. Thoughts have a frequency. Some could remain, like sound waves, until something shatters them or they dissipate over time. There are other possibilities we could consider, too, about the fellow you saw. He doesn't have to be a ghost."

"Let's just talk about ghosts at first, okay? They're an extension of the human. What's common to them that we agree on? Mine was in two places just like that," snapping her fingers.

Shelley leans forward, whispers huskily. "Maybe he didn't have to move because he was in the car with you."

"Then why didn't he get in the car with me the second time?"

"Maybe you had taken him where he wanted to go. Or maybe he did get in with you."

# ANNA

**He is here.** He stands by the other fireplace and the shadows there are displaced, accommodating his substance, whatever it is. He's drawn to beauty in sound and form. Not to me for that reason, because I'm plain except for my will, which is fancy enough. Yes, he shows me—yes, I am here. He is tall today, and broad-shouldered, and his hair is long, tied back, as my son preferred. He mouths, "She lies," leaving me to understand that Rachel has not told the whole story. I speak back. "Then I forgive her."

# DEBORAH'S STORY

**Deborah positions a** cane back chair before the fireplace, faces the women and dips in a shallow curtsy before seating herself in a formal pose, hands in lap and ankles crossed. This is a once-in-a-lifetime event and she will do her best to make it perfect. She closes her eyes briefly, shrugging the house down around her like a cape. She's as special for the house as it is for her. The traces of kerosene and candle wax tickle her nose. She feels their texture in her throat and deeper and takes a hanky from her skirt pocket in case she needs to cough. She has no doubt there are ghosts in attendance even if they're engaged in their own existence.

"Do you know the university's farm? I always wanted to stop there, because remnants of a stone building were visible in the woods opposite the entry road. One day this summer I decided to explore. No cars were parked by the main house. It was beautiful weather, sunny, with a nice stiff breeze now and then. When I walked into the woods, leaves came tumbling down as if I disturbed something.

The under canopy was dim, like a fine soot hung over the place. No bird sounds. I almost went back the way I had come, but this was right next to a major road, after all. I could see the foundation and the outline of rooms—burnt stones, charred wood, and uneven mounds of rubble. I paused appropriately, thinking of people who had lived in that home, and I mentally greeted them and explained my presence. I was wearing jeans, which is rare for me, and I had only a spade. Almost immediately I found a bottle—small, green glass, embossed, and full of bubbles. Very collectible. I was brushing off the fine particles that clung and it seemed that a dirt clod had fallen with them—fallen onto my hands and then from them. I looked up.

"A young man was not far away, partially hidden behind two white birches, the bark peeling like paper. I said, 'Who are you? What do you want?' He stepped into clear view without replying, but he tilted his head and smiled. 'You're scaring me,' I said. No answer. I got up, hurried for the road. He may have been behind me, but I didn't look, just went as fast as I could. Oh, stepping into the sunshine was precious, and the sight of my old car, and the university's big farmhouse itself. It was closer than my car, so I ran to the porch, rapped on the door. I called, 'Hello. Anybody here?' The door's upper half was clear glass, the border etched with flowers and vines. I could see the foyer, a small table with a dish for calling cards. I raised my eyes and there he was! I thought he was a reflection behind me but he was actually *before* me, in the house, by the table! I ran to my car, backed out to the main road, but I waited—just to see if he would emerge. He did. He came out, down the steps, and very quickly toward me. I left right then.

"I had a very bad night. I had forgotten it was Sunday afternoon. The farm shouldn't have been open. Monday morning, I phoned the campus office. The building was never open except by appointment and not that Sunday."

"What did he look like Deb?" Rachel asks. "You haven't said."

"Waifish, reddish-brown hair, a little curly. He wore a brown uniform, pants and jacket, nicely cut, not military."

"There was a murder in that stone house," Melody says. "A blind girl who used to sing at church functions lived there. She disappeared. All the windows were open, though the door was locked. And there was blood on one of the windowsills. There's an article about it in one of the historical society's records. People conjectured that if she had been killed in the dwelling, the murderer might have left the windows open, hoping something wild would come in and dispose of the evidence. Or if the girl had been trying to chase something out of the house, like a bird, something else came in. On the other hand, she may have just taken off with a boyfriend, to a better life. That's what I hope—that she got away. There's a children's song about her. It'll come to me."

"Maybe she's why I was alert that day," Deborah says. "She was around the farm grounds. I mean her ghost was. She was that dimness over the site, like ashes. Real fine. Oh. That makes me think of web ghosts! Anyhow, I sensed what she was feeling, like Melody or Connie said earlier. I don't like that idea either, Rachel. How awful if thoughts are floating around. What if one lodged in you?"

"It might seem like a possession," Connie says. "Might *be* a possession. Sorry, Rachel." Wine glass in hand, Connie shifts from the floor to an armless, green brocade chair. "This story is like Rachel's. It could be either type of haunting. The ghost doesn't speak to Deborah so she's possibly watching a replay—a residual haunting—but he's *aware* of Deborah, which makes it different, intellectual. He was going to get in the car with Deborah. The blind girl wouldn't have been driving. This was personal."

"But he wouldn't have hurt me, right? Couldn't?" from Deborah, heart-shaped face somber.

"Of course not," from Rachel.

# THE PANTRY
## MELODY

**Melody gives the** kitchen counter a speedy wipe down, rinses out the wine bottles, and shoves them safely into the trashcan, down toward the bottom. She's facing the closed pantry. It's such an odd pantry, and she knows something of old houses such as this one. She thinks of the many dramatic scenes in which the heroine does something exceedingly foolish. Melody doesn't desire to endanger herself, but the enticement to confirm what she suspects is strong. She opens the pantry door and feels a tinge of coolness, possibly caused by the movement of the door itself. She waits for that to cease. The draft continues. The shelves directly before her seem uneven, one side a little forward. With a finger she pushes lightly against the shelf nearest her. The wall creaks inward and to the left. She expected this, yet she is momentarily immobile, and terribly weak. Her heart throbs. Her legs tremble. Any excitement does this to her. The spell passes, and she wants to see, just one quick look. She determinedly steps forward. She can go either left or right. She's thrilled — one for the records! She's at the top of steep stairs descending on the right. She remembers the slanting storm door outside. A cellar or root cellar. She goes down slowly, holding her heavy skirt up ankle high and intermittently touching the damp wall for balance.

After the last step, turning cautiously to the right, she stands at the entrance, peering straight into it. It smells rank. A jagged rectangular aperture at the opposite end allows a hazy band of moonlight that widens to mid-room and makes almost visible the shapes below and around.

Something moves in the distant right corner. She whirls instinctively, clambers upward a few steps, feels her skirt caught, a tug backward. She jerks free and scrambles on, panting. She swings the panel shut, dashes from the pantry, and latches it closed. She rests against the counter, watching the pantry door. She's breathless, elated. She hears her friends' voices. Her chest is heaving but she's not truly afraid. It was a possum or raccoon, some small animal that had come through that opening. She pats her chest. If she tells the others about the cellar, which she should probably do, they'd all be down there or worrying about it, and have to sleep together, be up all night. For what? She can keep it to herself just overnight. And tomorrow, it'll be a real gift and they can look at everything together, with plenty of rest, and time to do things right. When her breathing slows, she strides into the great room.

"Kitchen's done," she says. "Coffee pot set for morning."

Melody knows the passage also led to the other side of the house. A secret passage isn't at all strange in this neck of the woods. This is a Civil War house, and many of them had spaces for concealing treasures, menfolk, womenfolk, children.

# FIRST NIGHT

## ANNA

**He waits for** them to take their beds. He stands by the
railing, his face toward me, my son's face, only I know that
set to the eyes and mouth. Not John. He turns away, offers
his back to me as he looks down into the great room. Is
this how your son stood that day? he is asking. Does this
recall your life? Your son's? Have at me, dear Anna. Here I
offer you the coward's blow.

"Monster," I say, and my words must make a sound,
a true one. I see Rachel come into the hall, look quizzically
toward me.

He is no longer near the railing, but he is not gone far.
William. Help me. Our boy is loose.

He was a sweet baby. He was good. Something
hungered for him, sought him. My boy. My baby. I think
the other had lived here long before we came.

I am in the hallway when they closet themselves away
from one another. I know he's among them, tasting fear and

natures like the dog of the universe. I speak to them, but they don't hear my words. Stay together, I tell them. Go home. It is not too late to flee. In the big bedroom, which the older one chose for herself, is a hat tree. William brought it for me from the city. Its bare, curving arms turn up, polished and smooth, and only five of the rounded tips hold hats. I had intended to fill it with bonnets from special days. There were too few. A blue hat, banded with a yellow ribbon, is so light a breeze could send it sailing. With both hands I cup the hat, lift up, up. The hat tumbles down and the woman rises, comes close. But she looks toward the hall where the little one, Shelley, now stands.

"Go," I say. "Go. You're in danger."

"Did you do that Shelley?" Connie says. "Move the hat? I think you did."

Shelley shakes her head, but she herself isn't sure.

I visit each room and attempt to see what each woman has brought with her, see more of her nature. I would open a suitcase, a drawer, but my hand passes through. In one room, Shelley's, is a tintype of Elizabeth. It belonged to my son and was not here before. I cannot lift it, but it seems that I do feel it, thumb to front, fingers to back. I try to leave my thoughts and touches on all I can, because even as ghost perhaps I have a scent or leave a mark, to claim ownership or announce power, to dissuade or encourage.

I cannot always see him, but I think he can always see me. I think he could absorb me if I weakened, make his future mine. I don't know where he is, which room, after which woman.

# BEDROOMS

## RACHEL

**In Rachel's room,** the wallpaper is blue, with a peach pattern, sprigs of some wispy flowers. The bed is canopied, has a thick, soft mattress, surely softer than was common back in those days, whenever those days were. The furniture is burled wood with gilt filigreed pulls — dresser, a writing table, and chair. She opens the table's single drawer, sees a few sheets of peach-colored paper and one folded sheet, blue. Even before she reaches for it, she knows it's a note, hopes it is.

> *A kiss for you, sweet Elizabeth, in word alone. I would prefer a way closer to my heart and yours.*
>
> *John Alan*

That's great. A good thing to find. She smells the paper. Is it old? Did they have colored paper? She returns the note to the drawer, pats it down fondly, and surveys the room. The beginning is all too perfect. She's wary. The note could easily be a prop. Many similar commercial hooks might be planted throughout the place, like that treasure of old newspapers downstairs. She doesn't want to act a fool or be fooled. She has to be very sharp. She owes it to the girls, too. They all have a stake in this. She takes a deep breath, feels the rise of her breasts and the tightening of her nipples. Maybe some guy named John Alan really had loved sweet Elizabeth and their ghosts loved on. Or love on—present tense. Great. Good for them.

She sits on the bed and begins shedding her clothing, peeling off first the black leggings, then the black cowlneck sweater. Static-electricity sparks sting her arms, and she shivers. The tilted mirror reveals her now-wild red hair, frizzing out witch-like, and makes her face flat and mongoloid. She doesn't like the image. She alters the mirror's angle. The gals don't know she was with a lover the night she saw the ghost fellow. She and a writer friend had agreed to meet in the back lot of the V-Village store just outside Clinton. She had gotten in his car. He had kissed her, said, "You sure about this?" "You bet," she had replied, untruthfully. She was riding nerves and heightened desire and kind of balancing on the edge of a sameness life or a completely changed one. If she went home, she was choosing good-old Rachel, faithful wife. That's what she should have chosen. She wasn't a good person. She didn't deny it.

It had been a crazy night. He growled and bruised his beard into her neck, breasts, belly, thighs, groin. The motel had a neon cowboy on the office roof and the light flickered, showing that lasso tossed every few seconds. She was figuratively roped, cornered, tied, had. And loved it. Then, she loved it. Afterward, he had lain with his cheek on her abdomen, his hand cupped over her groin, as if protecting her. He went to sleep briefly, she thought, and when he roused, he kissed her belly, said, "I envy your husband."

The last line had been a barb—unintentional, she believed, because he wasn't a bad guy. How could he envy her husband when she had just cheated on him? When the great sex had been with someone else?

"He's a good man," she said, honest about her husband and thus about herself. He didn't deserve what she was doing. For him, she wished she were a better person.

From there to the V-Village dark parking lot, her own car, and that strange ride, surreal, joy and guilt right in the car with her, drying every breath she took. The sudden sight of a guy by the road, and moments later having to pee. Wouldn't you know? Who caps off a torrid night with having to pee on a gravel road?

Then that weird young man again. She was convinced it was a single person. She had seen him after that night, standing under the streetlight outside her home. It had to be him. That loose brown garb. How could he have found her house? Maybe another young guy happened to be waiting for a ride, or lighting a cigarette, and she caught a glimpse of him at the precise angle that made him resemble the other one. Or her guilt created the resemblance. In which case she was going to see him the rest of her life because he appeared on the night she cheated. She clasps her head. *Rachel, stop it. Stop it.* She didn't believe she had picked up a memory, but, if she had opened a door, maybe things had come out, even thoughts. She shivers.

She didn't care if everything was random. Whatever power she had, she would use. She is here and on task. She digs in the blue duffel bag for her camera. She has multiple shots of the downstairs, including furnishings, her friends, and a video of part of Deborah's story. She's discreet. She doesn't make a big to-do about photos. She will most definitely write about this and maybe compile a documentary. She wants to have all she needs to illustrate the tone and events of the weekend. Is this compromising the actual goal of their group, just to share personal stories and to explore the house, interact with a ghost? Is she weakening the possibility of a sighting and interaction? She sits on the bed, trying to adjust this constantly driven, wavery self of hers. She closes her eyes, which seems brave, and opens them by tiny increments. "John," she says, "please don't be alarmed by my taking pictures. It's not to be invasive. I need them." She glances around the room, friendly and seeking. "Okay. Here goes." She takes multiple shots. If anything happens overnight, she won't have to rely on memory, especially memory in the midst of emotional turmoil.

She situates the camera on the round table by her bed, turns off the already dim light, and watches the layers of floating darkness.

Old phrases rise to her lips. *Matthew, Mark, Luke, and John, bless this bed I lie upon. Now I lay me down to sleep, I pray the Lord my soul to keep.* She shakes her head as if she would dispel what clings in memory. What she is, she is, and she will neither apologize nor ask forgiveness for it.

She is anxious to take charge, to do something, find something. Move on. Explore. She thinks of the tiny bedroom past hers. Different. She goes into the hall just as she is, in scant panties and bra. The cold air feels great. She opens the door, peeks in. "You in here?" she asks, and then enters, pads barefoot to mid-room. Her skin crawls with the energy around her. Such a spare room, only a small desk and narrow bed. She opens a closet, sees a few clothes, a box, shoes—canes? A creaking alerts her, and she darts to the door. "Oh no, you don't." Doors swing shut in every house, something to do with balance and drafts. She doesn't want to stay, though. It's like her guilt has unnerved her, is almost writhing the air. In the hallway, she closes the door behind her, falls against it, listening. The thought that something might actually speak her name chills her. In the morning, she'll look in the closet again, get that box. She walks to the stair landing to peer down into the great room.

The stairs look dusted in dry moonlight. Filmy. She wonders why she assumed the ghost would be John and not Elizabeth. What if it's Elizabeth's energy she feels? She tries to visualize a young woman on the stairs and sees, just for the briefest second, a shimmer of current. When it doesn't return, she blinks, scans the downstairs, and returns to her room. Maybe.

# MELODY

**What had she** seen in the cellar before she was startled? A raised area in the far-right corner, a black pipe near the south wall, stone and dirt floor. A boiler? A nagging something. She would worry it to the ground.

Dressed in a white flannel gown, as she would be at home and which should keep her warm, Melody breaks out in gooseflesh. She has brought a cup of tepid coffee upstairs with her and now sips from it. She trembles slightly and fears spilling coffee on the white sheets. She sets the cup on the night-table, avoiding the tatted doily, then plumps pillows to elevate her head and shoulders. She pulls the covers up to her waist. They seem to tighten over her feet and she wiggles her toes. This happens often when she's weary. She'll feel as if something creeps up the mattress or walks on tiny feet, like a cat or small dog — of which she has none. She understands this has, or could have, a physical cause. Exhausted muscles can contract almost imperceptibly and affect the mattress. Twitching travels, just as wind ripples water. A person isn't always aware of the origin. Other causes are possible, too. Tiny spasms in muscles can feel like touches.

The moving sensation comes again from beside her. She watches the spot. She's not afraid, just observant and cautious. It doesn't happen again. A letdown, really. She sips from the cup and contemplates speaking aloud. She's not quite ready for that. She doesn't *invite*. She hears Rachel's voice in the hall. That's reassuring. She's not alone. They're a team. She likes the sense of community, which is good since she has no children. She leaves the light on, scoots down, and readies herself to relax and sleep as much as possible. When she's really drowsy, she reaches out for the lamp chain, and tugs. Dark with floating dots. That wakens her thoroughly and she jerks the chain. Sleep will come easier with a light. Her husband would enjoy knowing about this. She doesn't frighten easily. At home, she sleeps in total darkness and even carries trash out at night. It's a weakness to need a nightlight. She remembers the yellow bone knife Ben gave her. She rises, takes the pretty thing from her tote bag of sundries, and lays it on the nightstand. She's sharing the experience with him. When she tells him about this, he will be very delighted, and so will she. It's a kind of gift.

# SHELLEY

**Shelley arranges her** few items into an empty dresser drawer. A lace scarf protects the dresser top, and on it are two photographs, one of a gaunt, handsome young man, maybe sixteen, and a girl of about the same age, a blonde, valentine beauty type, sweet face. She wears a white dress of many ruffles. Shelley reviews herself in the mirror. She's much that type of girl, only less confident. Not as pretty. The spidery glass veils her reflection. She is ghostly herself. She stops that train of thought. She surveys the room again, sees little tears in the wallpaper, a hole that could have once held a hook but probably isn't deep or wide enough to hide a camera—she's a modern woman and knows human behavior is often ugly. Men spy; people spy. She thinks about getting a chair and looking through the hole but is afraid for her eyes. She doesn't want to get excited or introspective. Nothing extreme.

She notices that her movement has shadowed across the photograph of the young man. She repeats the simple action. No shadow crosses the glass. She supposes it was just a flicker of the lamp. She turns in a slow circle, seeking any thicker dimness or shifting shadow. She takes her camera to the bed with her, sits down and begins unbuttoning her blouse as if readying for bed. The air right before her seems cooler. Then cold. Definitely cold. It seeks something. Her.

Deliberately slowing mind and body, she picks up her camera, opens the panel, which gives a gray screen, as if it filmed fog. She doesn't aim it directly before her. She makes no sudden or aggressive move. She is a quiet person. A meek one. She turns the lens toward the dresser to her left, raises it only enough to bring the mirror into the frame. She presses the button. Light flashes and she sees the cold in the mirror, like a halo of lamplight around a person, a man, not too big. Now she stands quickly, gripping the bedpost as she turns sharply and tightly toward the door, which she opens and then walks rapidly across the landing to the other wing. The first door is open. It's the big room, Connie's. It's empty.

She enters anyhow, goes across to a deep-blue wingchair with its back to the wide window. She sits down, facing the bed and the hall. An inner door opens, and Connie steps out. She's wearing pale green pajamas, her gray braid pinned up tight.

"Shelley. What's wrong?"

She doesn't want to tell it now, to bring it real into place.

"I'd like to stay in here, if that's all right."

"What happened?" Connie comes to sit on the bedside, nudging Shelley to move over. "I haven't seen anything. Obviously, you have."

"My room just got very cold. One of the signs."

"That's great. Let's check it out." She starts up, stopped by Shelley's protest.

"No. Not yet. Please. The whole house is cold. I'm nervous and overreacting. I shouldn't have intruded. You said you could share."

"I will. Happy to. Let me check the room for you, though. We should do that. We shouldn't ignore things and I don't want to."

"Please don't. It's my room. Promise you won't."

"Really? I hate to let it go." Connie stands, gestures to the bed. "Sure, you can sleep here. I'm going downstairs to get some water and to look around. Will you be okay alone?"

"Yes. It's not a good idea to go down there by yourself."

"Why?"

"It's too far away from the rest of us."

"That's why I want to go. If something's around, I want to be available." Her eyes question Shelley. "Do you think I'm in danger?"

Shelley thinks of the brief contact moments ago. She shakes her head no.

"Damn," Connie says softly, smiles, and walks away,

around the bed. "I trust you to know." She tucks something from the nightstand into her pajama pocket and leaves with one reassuring glance back.

Shelley flips out the camera screen. She did get him. It could just be the spidered mirror or a reflection from the wallpaper. She can't recall the wallpaper and it isn't visible in the photo. She holds a picture of cold with a face, as if a part of the room, right in the center, was icing up, and she caught its reflection. She remembers the woman who had gotten into a camera once and showed her face on the photos. Shelley has the urge to delete the photo now, before the ghost can take up residence. It might be too late. She thinks of her suitcase in the other room. Could she take home a whole family of them? She doesn't know. She lets the thought pass. This photo, though, is a contribution to the weekend, to her companions. She has something to offer. She will share as they do, slowly. She wants to be one of the others. Not singled out. Not strange. Lonely. She snaps the camera shut and slides it under the blue chair.

She gets on Connie's bed and stares at the doorway. The hat-tree arms overlay the stair rails beyond and form a maze of small, hovering tunnels. She tries to refocus and dispel the illusion, then just observes it. She concentrates on her heartbeat. She is present in this world. Her heart beats. She breathes.

# DEBORAH

**Deborah's heart is** tripping a little, but she isn't afraid because ghosts might *frighten* someone, and be dangerous for the *timid*, but they wouldn't *kill* anyone. They could tip the balance at a dire moment, cause a bad decision. She supposes. She thinks of the adult kiss by the boy in *The Turn of the Screw*. Inappropriate, precocious. Evil? Maybe. Tawdry. Now this experience, her own, is truly grand, or could be. Her room on this night, a night out of how many? A lifetime. Let it be memorable. Not too frightening. The wardrobe is catercorner to the bed. She moves to open it, warily, a tenuous grip on the round, polished handles. What if something waits? Really does? She takes a breath, yanks the doors toward her. They stick and she has to yank harder, one side giving first, baring the emptiness while she wrestles with the stuck panel. She pushes them together, and one swings out. She has to hold them just so, ease them in place. There is no latch or spring. They hold together simply by tension and might fall open easily since the floor isn't even and tight—the boards squeak beneath her.

She seeks the best vantage point for the camcorder, the widest angle. She shortens the tripod to its smallest height, about eight inches, and attaches the camcorder. Dragging the one chair in the room over to the wardrobe, she sets the apparatus atop the wardrobe, at the edge, and angles it down till she is certain it will catch a wide swath of the room. The best place might be in her *hands,* so she could film what she sees, but this angle might capture what she can't or doesn't see. She has her own eyes *from* the bed and the camera eye *on* the bed.

She dons a white cotton gown away from the camera's scope and, as she slips into bed, smooths the garment down. This scene might eventually be for public viewing because of a ghost's presence. She is somewhat fevered. In movies, the women always brave the most foolhardy act because they are meeting the audience's expectation, not their own call for self-preservation. She isn't under *threat.* Ghosts don't kill. They hint and nudge and play against the sensitivities of the person. According to some of Shelley's comments tonight, they come into being *through* that sensitivity.

Now, that worries her, just a little. She remembers the deafening knocking in the halls of Hill House, scratchings, the distortion of structures. All that caused, likely, by the unconscious misery and longing of one woman. The memory is so close, Deborah's stomach and heart soar together and she gasps. She will turn out the lamp in a minute. Oh. A shadow just swam across the ceiling. She wads the gripped sheet top nervously, tugs it up under her chin. The light is going to stay on for a while. That doesn't hurt anything. She's not ready to invite something in the dark.

She has forgotten to turn on the camcorder! Eventually, that practical problem focuses her breathing. She scurries over, steps onto the chair, and pushes the button without having to lift the camera down. She has used it often enough with her students. She fairly hops the short distance to the bed. The red light on the camera is reassuring. Working.

At some point she falls asleep. She wakes rather suddenly, listening for something. The lamp is off. The red light continues. By the wardrobe is a shadow, as tall as the wardrobe. She worries that it can sense her breathing, see the slit of eye she must be revealing. Her mouth trembles. She can't move. She's in the midst of a nightmare. Something lowers over her and she doesn't want to fight.

# CONNIE

**Connie loves this** aloneness, now, past midnight. A kind of whisper silence inside and outside, too, a permanent aloneness. It could be the dawn of a forever day. The house looks misty, filled with dreams. She lingers on the red davenport. She speaks internally because a voice could shatter possibility. *You are here, aren't you? You see me, hear me. You hear us all. Will you respond to me if I persist? Or am I the wrong kind of being? Do you communicate with only one kind? Rachel? Shelley? All of them but me?* She imagines a sudden touch to the nape of her neck, or a sudden coldness, and wants it even as she thinks the real occurrence might kill her. In one pocket is the small recorder, which she turns on, just in case. In the other pocket is the curved vial of brewed-down salvia. She could sip some now and induce an experience, show her willingness to be privy to some other world. Maybe it would make her ready. She is too staid, ugly, and old to entice a mystery alone. Unworthy. Even victims have some allure.

A splotch of light slides across the richly patterned

rug and her eyes snap to the window. Where did that come from? Had a moonbeam just found a crack in the night? She peers. Shadow layers flow. Is her vision, too, slowing? No longer reliable? Barefoot, so aware of her own presence, she goes into the shallow kitchen. The coffee is set for the morrow. She could empty the salvia into that water, and then, in the morning, watch the brief transformation that effected. She could help the others have an experience, something to remember, to write about. Infuse them with a different kind of spirit. Nope. Not her place to do that, nor her nature. Just thoughts. The life of the mind.

She takes her medication and one alprazolam.

As she heads back to the stairs, she hears music, violin, quick and light. She's unsure it *is* music. It could be something else, distorted by the weather or by her own desire. It's like water music. Rain. Beautiful. Fanciful. She sits on the yellow settee, looks behind her because she doesn't want anything to creep up on her, though she does want him to appear.

"I know that tune," she offers to what might be present. "'Four Marys.'" The music ceases, which is like a direct answer, a no-voice answer. "It's beautiful." She waits. "Please play it again." The music doesn't begin, but the room changes. The air is starker, as if a dim light has glowed it up evenly, even the nooks and crannies. Something that can fill the whole space. She feels closed in on, too, and has difficulty breathing. "I'm not as boring as you think," she says. She feels complicity with the ghost. Maybe the others feel the same. Loneliness is not a sin. She goes up the stairs slowly, turning only once, and fearfully, boldly, too, to look behind her, wanting just a suggestion, a glimmer, of someone there. On the landing, she cues the recorder backward a few seconds, and, with the volume low, holds it to her ear as it replays. There it is! She got the music! Only a little of it, but enough.

In her room, she sits on the bed gingerly, watches the vague blackness outside the windows. She can hear Shelley's regular breathing. The young woman's nature is odd. Shelley's attempt to appear simple is pretty transparent. She's a disconcerting, strong presence and certainly restraining some kind of power. Maybe she honestly doesn't know it.

Connie thinks of the music. A ghost had been with her—somewhere in the room. Watching her. She picks at the covers, longing to regain and hold the memory, the moonlight, the shiver of pleasure. She knew the tune. What could that mean? Her body has another memory and anticipates the pills' effect. A weakness overtakes her arms, then legs. This is a kind of preparation, like practicing for the big event. Death. Women survive tragedies better than men because they have practiced many times over, worrying in advance, fearing and grieving in advance. That is a truth in the real world.

Her thinness is a boon here, since she doesn't move the mattress much, just lowers herself like a remnant of old hurt. Shelley sleeps on or seems to. The memory of the music, whatever its source, plays in the room for Connie. She tugs the quilts up and gives in to the sweet onset of sleep.

# SATURDAY,
# DAWN

# MELODY

**The sun has** begun its ascent in the east, yet the sky lightens very little, keeping the house and grounds in a sluggish predawn. Brief gusts bring flicks of cold rain. Names of the deceased are roughly chipped into the headstones, shallow and difficult to read. Melody, kneeling on the cold earth, holds a sheet of vellum paper over one section of an inscription and rolls a piece of brown chalk over the words. The wind flutters the free corners of the paper. Photos would be easier, but this is personal and records different nuances, intimate. She can take photos later, or someone will. She feels a drop of water, another, throws her head back to look at the sky. Something really bad is coming in. She puts the sheet in the folder with the unused ones, closes the flap, and struggles up. Only two headstones have dates, mid 1800's pre-Civil War. The name on all was Bledsoe. She vaguely remembers a Bledsoe in the county histories. The man, a physician, had been unable to save his family from some blight. A fever? Something. And here they lie. This soil may be diseased.

She hears a thin screech, like an old gate, and sees the storm door rising. She continues standing just long enough to recognize the man emerging—the caretaker, Luke Essex. She doesn't understand why he's here but doesn't want to confront him. Maybe he forgot to do something with the boiler. It's strange, disconcerting. She squats down behind a headstone. He's running in the opposite direction, toward the front, past the porch. He must have left his truck along the highway below. That's what she had almost known last night. Luke had been in the cellar, lying down in the dark far corner. He was probably going to spook them if they ventured down there. Could be he sleeps in the cellar whenever he wants. It wouldn't surprise her. Bums roam the countryside around most towns and have favorite empty buildings they inhabit. Even churches lock their doors now. One church in Mason has a digital lock code for night-time access. This sneaky behavior, however, doesn't fit Luke Essex's reputation. He's a quirky, good fellow. At the society's dances, he lets the other musicians carry a couple waltzes so he can take an elderly woman or two for a gentle turn on the dance floor. He's a thoughtful person.

A few more cold drops, and yet perspiration dots her temples and the deep cleavage of her breasts. Feeling lightheaded, she stands slowly, not to worsen dizziness, and steadies herself by gripping the headstone. She often suffers from vertigo. Soon, her body rallies and she's back to business, admiration of the place, the desire to ready the kitchen and prepare breakfast for the others.

She puzzles over the name Mary Bledsoe, which reminds her of another name close to the surface of her memory. It, too, is an M B name. She can almost say it, wants to spit it out. It will come to her suddenly, as those things do, when she isn't trying.

A faint warmth crosses the dip of breast at bodice rim. It repeats, as if someone is blowing there. She starts toward the house, breathless.

# SATURDAY MORNING, GREAT ROOM

# THE WOMEN

**At the oak** table, the women pass Deborah's camcorder around. The tiny screen shows the air in her room shimmering and there's a muffled sob. Her dark shadow form struggles up, reaches for the lamp, and the resulting glow reveals her dazed, fearful expression. She looks drugged, actually, and unsure of her surroundings. She tugs a pillow close, scoots back against the head of the bed, peering about the room warily.

"What happened, Deb?" Rachel asks. "Something scared you. What?"

"A nightmare. I have them often. I can't open my eyes or speak or move. I hate them, hate them. I was told I could learn to wake myself. I could think about it before I go to sleep, how the dream may come and what I'll do. The other option," she rolls her eyes, "which is no option, is to let the dream happen."

"You may think it was a nightmare, Deborah, but it looks like something was in your room. See this?" Connie points to the screen. "You're blocked from view like the camcorder loses power and then suddenly you're visible again, crying your eyes out."

"Nothing happened to me," Deborah insists hoarsely. "I had a bad night, but I know what it was. I have a sleep disorder, sleep paralysis, and it's worse when I'm not at home. I'll feel something is in the room that I can't see. I'm afraid it will speak or I will see it, but that never happens. Last night was the same. I don't recall sitting up, but if my breathing gets bad, I have to, and we've been burning lots of candles and wood."

Her face is puffy, eyelids swollen, and the fresh eyeshadow like moth dust. Her lips look bruised.

"You don't believe a ghost was in your room?"

"No. I was ill."

"I know for certain we have a ghost." Connie sets a silver, slender audio recorder on the table. "I want you to listen to this until the tape is over. You'll hear more than one kind of sound." She switches the control on.

There is a faint swishing, like distant, steady waves, a white noise meant to sleep by, more like the machine's motor. Then comes a tsking from a human voice, or human-like, *tsk, tsk, tsk,* like trying to get something's attention, *tsk, tsk,* the tongue against the roof of the mouth. It varies, alternates between that *tsk, tsk* and a click in the back of the throat, as if clucking to hens or to a team of horses, only more slowly, with different intent. The *tsk* again, louder, as if the maker of the sound sees the machine, leans near, *tsk, tsk, tsk,* and changes the word, *shuh, shuh, shuh, sweet-y, sweet-y. Shuh, shuh, sweet-y. Shuh. Shuh.*"

"Jesus."

Connie shakes her head, index finger across her lips.

A harsh sound, like a snort.

Connie's expression says *stay quiet.*

After long seconds, another sound: A violin, very thin, strained. When that ceases, Connie picks up the machine, switches it off. "I heard only the music. I didn't hear the vocal sounds till I played it."

"What do you think it was?" from Rachel.

"I want it to be paranormal, of course, and it must be, because none of us made this." She waves the small recorder. "Evidence. We have Deborah's video and this music and . . . voice. There's a ghost here — or something."

"I hate to disappoint you, Connie," Melody says, "but I know the source of the music and it wasn't a ghost. It was a guy in the cellar. The caretaker. Luke Essex. I saw him leaving the cellar this morning. He must have slept down there last night. He didn't have a fiddle with him. I bet he had a recorder to play while he made the other noises. He was priming the pump."

Dismay alters Connie's features. "Why would he do that?"

"Maybe someone suggested it. Not anyone from the historical society, though it might make the house more popular. A prank? Maybe Luke just wanted to give us what we were looking for."

"I hate that," Connie moans. "I don't want that to be true of him."

"You also don't want to lose your ghost music," Melody says. "Or your ghost. Neither do I, but we have what we have."

"I'd rather think he was guarding us," Connie says. "I don't want to doubt everything that happens."

"I'm disappointed, too." Melody begins clearing the breakfast settings. "I don't know what he was doing." She pauses, holding the stack of paper plates and napkins. "I did find something you'll all want to see. I want to see it, too. A hidden passage behind the pantry."

"Oh, Jesus," Rachel says, bounding up. "I knew it, Melody. I knew something happened to you last night. I found some stuff, too, in that little bedroom. Nothing like a passage. Where? The kitchen? You should have told us."

Deborah, listless, taking a slow breath before following the others, sees a serpentine movement in the rug's pattern near her. She blinks. It's not in the rug, but on it, a delicate gold chain and a very tiny cross. She thinks it might belong to one of the girls and picks it up, drops it into her vest pocket, and hurries after the others.

# PART II

# SATURDAY,
# MIDMORNING
# THE PASSAGE

**For the few** moments the women are all inside the passage, they together sense the cellar to one side, like a drop-off, not sheer, since there are steps, and it seems like a well, brings back vague memories of a time near a dank, familiar, almost nostalgic smell—fruit cellars, storm cellars, unfinished basements, cisterns, too, and damp barns, and water tanks, even mud pies, memories not distinguishable so much as a lifetime of feelings. In the opposite direction the passage rises slightly, ramp-like, and they see it will run along the back of the kitchen and dining room, then perhaps open left. The passage glows dimly from the spill-light of the kitchen and pantry and needles of light through the outer wall. It's a goldish tint at the moment, and they realize that's because the flooring of the ascending passage is a dark gold, cloth-like burlap, drawn taut, yet supple, as if it has been oiled many times, and well trodden.

"I can't do it," Connie announces. She has been positioned all along a little closer to the pantry, keeping a foot forward enough to block the swinging shut of the panel, which she has consciously pictured and guards against. "I want to." She gives in to the impulse to run and simply steps free of the passage and into the pantry, like she's exiting a plane after an arduous trip. She exhales in relief and shakes her head. "I had no idea I'd balk at this."

Deborah follows her. "I'll keep Connie company," she says sheepishly.

"That's okay," Rachel says. "You two keep watch. If we run into trouble, you can rescue us."

"You can count on it," Connie says.

"Just keep this open."

The passage is about four-feet wide, and the three walk in a staggered single file. Melody, with wrist light gleaming, has taken the lead, and Shelley the rear. At the corner, a ripple of whistle sounds, followed by Connie's soft laugh, and they look back. The pantry light forms a distorted, angled gate, not too distant and thus reassuring. They go on, left. The pinprick holes are on both sides now and the women pass through slivers of cool air and light. The incline continues. The inner wall reaches high enough to accommodate the domed ceiling of the great room on the other side. They realize a complete second floor is only over the front of the house. Above them now are heavy rafters and dark gaps. Melody switches off the wrist light to verify that the flooring itself glows a little, then switches it on again. A few feet farther, they arrive at the highest part of this passage, closed on the left by ladder steps going steeply up.

"That would take us above the bedrooms," Rachel says. "It might be crawl space only, edging over the landing, and then to the other wing."

"Or to an attic," Shelley says. "There could be different attic rooms, the way the roof is pitched, different turns and widths."

The passage continues to the right, narrower, darker, a wall. Abutting the wall, not quite visible, something like striated shadows. Steps. Steep and shallow. Six of them, ending at what could be, and must be, a door.

"Where exactly are we?" Rachel says.

Melody answers. "Probably just beyond our bedroom wing."

"Past the little bedroom?"

"Yes. That's where we should be. Past the wall. What do you think, Shelley?"

"Yes. We're past the wall. I think this is a servant's room."

Rachel tries the metal knob. It doesn't give. She twists harder, putting shoulder to the door, too, to loosen it. She hears and feels crackling in the knob as it turns. The panel doesn't budge. "We need a crowbar," she says. "Something to pry. Or a hammer. It's nailed shut."

"We can't damage the place, Rachel," Melody says. "It's not our property."

"I'm not leaving the door closed."

"There may be nothing on the other side."

"You know better. I'm getting in there, alone if I have to. I'll pay for any damages, I promise. Don't you want to know? How can you not?"

They can't persuade Rachel to come with them. "I'll be fine," she insists. "You two be careful. Remember, turn left when you see the ladder, then it's a straight shot down and turn right."

# DEBORAH

**Deborah feels off,** as if she's contracted something. Nauseated, a tremor in her muscles, and an ugly taste in her mouth. It's difficult to think of choices and fulfilling your obligations when your body rebels. Except for the fact that she's ill, she would actually like to be with the others, exploring, maybe discovering something rare and meaningful. She eyes the passage entry again. She recalls a great story about souls lost between walls, spreading word against oppression, warning the living. They don't know they're dead and their corpse eyes have been pecked out by birds. The souls still *see*. She wishes she hadn't remembered the piece.

The kind of ghost she desires would be a gentleman, something like the sea captain of Mrs. Muir, who loved her enough to absent himself so she might have a rich life. "I shall go away until I have learned greater wisdom," he said. Mrs. Muir longed for him, as Deborah longs for someone. The captain was mannerly, masculine, very masculine. Such a deep longing was the undoing of the governess in *The Turn of the Screw*. Poor young woman. The governess loved the children's uncle. He was busy scouring the world for pleasure, with money and freedom and charm, and he simply passed his duller obligations, everyday chains, to the young governess, who turned all her desire for him, her desire to be valued, and to be accomplished, and to be active and courageous, turned it all into servitude to accept his responsibilities. And what did she receive in return? A little boy's sick kiss and a descent into madness.

Deborah yearns for a ghost who doesn't wait for her death, who escorts and rescues her. The one she saw at the university farm, if a ghost at all, was a boy-man who might have wanted to *rape* her.

She touches her tender and bruised lips. She had bitten them as she slept. It was a bad episode. One of the worst, like something sank into her whole body, took the very breath from her, turned her dry to death. Hot. Dry and hot. Dry and hot. She had struggled futilely to cry out. She feels sour.

The passage is quiet. What if her friends have been done away with somehow, and Deborah is here alone? The mood in the house itself is heavy, as if the sky has lowered into the upper parts and presses down. It's like the nightmare in daytime, pressing over everything. She feels feverish, has a rush of fear mingled with desire, like an overpowering nostalgia. She smells something both sweet and acrid. She grabs the car keys Rachel had left on the kitchen counter, hurries through the mudroom, onto the back stoop. Sharp air assaults her nostrils. She feels a few frigid drops on her scalp and hands. She surveys the field, the winter trees not too far, the back corner of the house, and goes on to the car, looking down toward the highway. Below is a man with a dog, trudging toward the woods, away from her. He wears a gold coat or hunting vest. His presence is both alarming and reassuring. There is no horizon to the west. Just gray, like a sheet of fog arriving. She could call her husband and be walking away at the same time. Oh, the small, boring, dear man. He would come to save her and take her away from this place. She could leave without interrupting the experience Rachel wants. True? No. That might ruin it for everyone. Still, she takes her phone from her coat pocket, punches the talk key. No service. Never any service! She stows the phone, pokes fingers into her vest pocket and brings out the chain and cross. If it's a message, it must be a safe one, and she's not going to ignore it. She wants to be a brave spirit and keep up with the girls.

# RACHEL

**Rachel is proud** of herself for remaining here, safeguarding that locked door while Melody and Shelley fetch tools to open it. If anything noteworthy is going to happen, she's not going to miss it. She should have brought her camera. This whole residence could be a setup. There could be only a blank wall behind the door. Whatever it is, she's a witness, a first-person account. This is what she's made of. She will stay here until she turns to stone rather than leave that door locked. She tries again. She leans into the door, shoving as hard as she can, balanced with one foot on the top step and the other leg bent against the door. There's nothing to grip for leverage. She has that feeling, being watched. She turns around. The dark here is like murky water.

"Are you there?" She waits a few seconds. "Come on. Make a sound, a sign. Say my name. It's Rachel."

The complete silence now seems deliberate, an affront to her daring. She sits down as well as possible, elbows on knees, her smooth, butterscotch hands dangling. Rachel wants a ghost to be here, some gain to match her efforts and irritation. Frustration rises. A thought comes that something might take her hand. She tries to force that thought away. She wants to fold her hands against her abdomen but leaves them loose. She squirms involuntarily. *Don't mess with me. Don't mess with me, buster. If you're here, step up to the plate.* She gnaws her lower lip. Her eyes read the dark in slow sweeps.

"There's something in this locked room, isn't there? Does it belong to you? Do you belong to it?" *We don't mean any harm,* she thinks. Her mind and mouth aren't in sync.

She can't get herself to settle down into what she should do. Genuinely invite the ghost. Make it feel safe. Here pinpoints of light on the outer wall and far above fade into undulating darkness. The step is as hard as cement, and shallow. She's uncomfortable. She tries to scoot backward and her movement brings a swirling in the dark.

"You *are* there, aren't you? A little timid?"

She tries to see it. She touches her chest above the heart, and speaks slowly, as if to be better understood. "I'm Rachel. Who are you?"

She hears a soft *whuff,* like a breath in or out, and presses with all her spirit against the door, seeking without wanting to a few inches more of retreat.

If something lurks there, in the syrupy dark, it is now catercorner from her, about four feet from the lowest step — a yellowish transparency, swimming into shape. Or is she simply extracting the lightest shade of black to make a shape — the *need* to see making the *seen*? It hunkers down, doesn't it? Now alters, thinning upward till the hint of face is at a level with hers, only feet away. Round black eyes. Is it a shape, truly? She feels it draw her, feels an odd comfort, and yet her skin tightens, she sweats. She resists. If it is not a ghost, what does she have to say to it? She has a strong urge to close her mind, to bury her thoughts. It's not possible. They're bubbling. *I'm not on your side, either. Fight it out yourselves.* All she wants is something better than average, not to be a little Midwest housewife, grow meat and potatoes fat, lose the proper verb, save her best clothes for the day she's going anywhere other than Walmart. Oh, oh. Isn't she better looking and smarter than any of the women she knows? Is it wrong to call herself what she is? To know she's better than what she has? Was rolling in the sack with a married man better? She almost cringes. Whew! Flail her arrogance. Cut off her nose. Stone her in the main street of town. Thank her lucky stars she's in a modern, western country even if she's in the conservative ditch. *I am Rachel and I am by God worth more than I have. Get thee behind me you creeping stink.*

"Are you a ghost?" she blurts.

Quiet, like the darkness gone void, all sound sucked into the heavens. She hears something, like a human voice breathed instead of spoken.

"More."

Her heart clenches, beats a heavy, slow beat, then quicker, quicker. There is no place for her to run. She has begged for a response and freely offered her name.

It is male. Without a doubt. Male. The presence is powerful, in her nostrils, ears, mouth, pores. It will steal her away, cut her out of time and into a place she doesn't know, will never know, cannot bear. She feels that happening.

"Rachel," she hears, a most wondrous sound. "Rachel! We're coming." Melody.

# JOHN

**She doesn't go** to meet them. She stays near me with her face down. Not so haughty now.

I could have opened the door at any time since Anna fastened it against me and the rest of the world. How bony she was, a passionate skeleton, all atremble. The greatest pleasure would be if she, Anna, opened it to me. She must hear them. She knows they will crack the temple. What will she do? I await Anna, dear, the knowing.

I listen at the door. I could take man shape if I chose. Anna is on the other side. Would she fall against me, into me? Do I feel the pulse of her fear? She is tiny, was ever tiny. Her husband was a boulder. I could be bigger. Huge. Shadow the house. Shadow the entire countryside. She was human. Loved something impossible to mimic.

Her bones could be scattered, ground to powder, burnt to ash.

*I love the door, that she would seal it. Such will.*
*Love.*

# ANNA

**I must leave** a message for these women. I dip my pen in the inkwell, lower it to the paper. Thoughts surge but I strain with this simple, simple task. Write, Anna!

I can't. I scratch at words.

Bury son. Bless.

I look toward my form on the bed. There's no longer sorrow in viewing myself. Freckles on the bridge of my nose, blunt fingertips. I think not of what I was but of what surrounded me. Tall sunflowers, their broad faces following the sun. Larkspur, so blue it hurt the eyes. The graceful bow of sudden lilies. Wind through my son's hair. His laugh. My husband, William.

My bones were always small and there was little flesh on them even before I lay down, ready to die, willing to die, but loath at the necessity of it. Now what power do I have? Could I take these crosses with me? I think of the cross I gave to Deborah and wonder if it is here, too, on that body. My body.

What will they do with me?

The women worry at the door and in spite of myself I retreat to the window as if I were flesh. I am afraid. I was afraid before, when I lay dying, and weeping, too, because I had killed my son and myself and left us to the unknown with such sin on both our souls, and that monster reigning in the house and perhaps the world. Now I risk another unknown.

I chide myself: You take hold. All that is good, and holy, and pure, and just, and praiseworthy. Think on these. Be brave. Be courageous. Be your best. Let them in. I approach the door and speak. "Let this door open to any that are good of heart. Or would be. Or would be good." Their women's voices murmur like water over rocks. I repeat: "Let this door open to any that are good of heart or would be good."


The women pound steadily at the door's rim until it loosens, hangs from the hinges. I expect him to surge in and drown me in infinite loss. There is no relief from fear. I back away, look at my former self on the bed. Will she frighten them? She used to be a little handsome.

They see the bed. See me. Murmur. Shelley edges through, slides to the side, remains against the wall near the door. She watches my body then slowly scans the room, stops her gaze at where I stand, her pale blue eyes like mirrors reflecting sky. Rachel maneuvers herself through, steps back for Melody.

"My God," Rachel whispers. "It's a corpse. It really is."

Such will they one day be. Gone, and perhaps alone, with a voice no one hears and a pain no one shares.

They study my sanctuary in quick glimpses that gradually slow. It is humble, but it is mine, fashioned to my purpose. Let them not disdain it.

"I didn't anticipate this," Rachel says.

"No." Melody shakes her head. "Not this. If it's real, and I think it is, I don't believe I can stand it."

We remain where we are. This is mine. This is all that is left to me. You are in its midst and you are mute? What word do you await? Help.

Shelley walks toward the bed. "She's real." She stares down at my face, at the length of my body. Her left hand hovers above mine as if she might take it. I am grateful for the gesture. She is a dear girl. "She's been dead a very long time." She comes to the window nearest me. We are inches from each other. She pulls back the curtain on the window. "A cross is in this window, probably in the others, too." She faces me directly, her pale eyebrows in a puzzled frown. She extends her hand forward and it passes through my forearm.

I love the intimate acknowledgment here, in my own space, with no language between us, plane to plane.

She doesn't reveal me to them. Perhaps she doesn't

really know what I am. Or that I am.

"There's a Bible by the bed," Shelley says. "And a cross on the door. She was protecting herself."

"She's been here a hundred years or more, probably since the Civil War." Melody approaches. "Hiding from soldiers of one side or the other." She looks at my stockinged feet, comes around to bend over my face. Her own hands are behind her back, lest she touch me, touch anything. "She's sort of preserved. I don't understand how that could be." She stands erect. "I feel like I've had the sense knocked out of me. I don't know what we have to do now."

"Neither do I," Rachel says. "I guess if we leave, we have to go to the authorities. We should call them." She shrugs. "I haven't had phone service for a while, and besides, a few hours won't matter to her, huh? We shouldn't rush out of here. We can inspect the place. We need to do that. We also need a camera. Could we get one? Go down and come back?"

"No." Shelley.

"We have to get pictures," Rachel asserts. "Of her, the whole room, before others come in. Police or whatever."

They open my few drawers quietly as if they might wake me. As in one sense they have. They open the trunk where I stored my own tools. Hammer and nails. The dried pastes that insured my dying. Our dying. They find, too, something I had forgotten, the evidence of my wasting away.

It was difficult to stay clean. I did. I did until I couldn't.

"These rags and . . . stuff," Melody says, "could probably be tested for what killed her. Especially the contents of these little jars."

"Hey." Rachel has found my attempted note. "Scratches. Nothing legible, damn it."

"Had to be her." Melody.

Rachel nods, again studies the body on the bed. "I wonder what she wanted to say. I want to know." She lifts the cap of the inkwell, sticks the pen down and raises it. "Ink. It hasn't dried up. You know that's impossible."

"Maybe it had some sort of oil or wax that got liquid in warm weather."

"It's not warm, Melody. The opposite."

"Then somebody brought it up here recently."

"Or made it in this very room."

"It's not blood." Shelley has lifted the lid of the inkwell. "Blood has a smell." She replaces the lid. It is shaped like a bird, rests firmly in the nest.

The ink is from berries. Raspberries. Near this house. I picked them and John walked with me, as if guarding me from the other. But the other was himself. When was that? When could I have made ink that still flows? I try to recall. He was taller than I, dressed in his favorite garb, that brown suit with the tiny stand-up collar, piping along the edges.

That was an autumn. He held a bowl into which I

placed the berries. He carried the bowl into the house. He started a fire in the big stove and we boiled the berries. The water was red. I tried to strain it. My hands shook and he took my hands in his, held them together, kissed them. He took the straining cloth. "Let me." The cloth turned white and dry.

"Which are you," I said.

"Your son."

"My son couldn't do that."

"He can now."

He. He. My son would have said "I."

"Look at me," he said. "Look."

I was going to do it. I wanted to see, be assured, know that he was sometimes completely separate, completely. I could someday save him.

"I love my son, more than life itself," I said. "Do you hear me, John? Be good. Try, sweetheart. Hold on to the good in you."

The sun was low then. I finished the chore and cleaned the kitchen. I must have. He stood near and talked about things we had seen together—a yellow bull charging across the field toward where we sat on a fence. Waxwings flying arcs up and back down like air blossoms. With a matchstick he had dipped in the ink he drew a flower on the back of my hand. I feared it. I thought I must scrub it off when he was gone.

He offered me the cup of ink and I accepted.

"Hold tight," he said. "Want to keep it. Believe you can."

When was that? I made the ink and yet can't use it? Was he teaching me? Who was teaching me? I don't want that other creature to love me.

I look at myself on the bed. My skin is unmarked. What he did to this self does not alter that form.

"We can tell Connie what's in here," Melody says, "but if we tell Deborah, we'll have to leave. She'll be scared to death. I'm more than a little shaky myself."

"So we don't tell Deborah," Rachel says. "I don't know about Connie. If either one of them asks for information, we can tell them we found a bedroom. We don't have to mention the . . . body. It's a temporary lie of omission. This woman has been dead a long, long time. A few more hours can't matter. I doubt Deborah will question us much. She doesn't want to know anything really scary."

Beyond them is the swirling black passage. Has he gone where the other two women wait or does he lurk in that dark? Will he enter now at will? What am I to do?

"Let's prop the door up," Shelley says. "She wanted to be locked in, and we can't leave her like this."

They maneuver the broken wood slab upright in the opening. Shelley hangs the cross on the nail that held it before, then slips through the gap to the others.

"That's the best we can do," I hear spoken loudly. Shelley.

I believe she speaks to me.

They are leaving now, Melody with her wrist light illuminating their pathway. "We found a shorter way by accident," Melody says. "We got lost but could hear Connie in the music room and she heard us. There's a secret entry. We told her what we found. She agrees Deborah shouldn't know. Not yet."

I am with them, last, behind Shelley. She half turns, sensing me.

"When we get back" Rachel says, "let's go through the old newspapers. We can get Deborah involved in that. We'll just be searching for any history about this house— the passageway. You know. We don't have to mention the lady upstairs. We need to find everything we can."

They don't have to mention me. I am their secret now. Not as it should be, but I might do the same. Is it to protect their own desire or to spare another's fear? Choices can stifle action, misdirect—two needs, two truths, opposing. Maybe there's never just one right, only a greater power.

As they bend to enter the music room I see him in the darkness, close, waiting for me.

"Anna," he says, and the tone is warm and sweet enough that I pause, even knowing he will lie. "I could enter your room at any time."

"I don't allow you."

"It's my affection for you that keeps me out. I obey your will."

"I know both as lies."

"I obey your will in many ways, in those that concern your own self. That is the best I can do. Now. I may learn. I learn from you."

"Leave my son. He's wretched. I'm wretched. Leave us."

"Do you really wish that? To be left where you are as you are?"

"Where is that?"

He stands so near I cannot see his face without looking up and I will not. His presence diminishes me. I feel encircled by blackness.

He stoops to speak in my ear though his thoughts are enough. "I can tell how you came to be here and where William is and why."

I can't answer. My wits have left me. He does tell stories. I recall. That William abandoned me of his own accord. With another. They drove away in a carriage. She was fair and young. A robust girl. I slip through the panel into the music room as the others did and hurry to find them.

# *JOHN*

**The brave one,** *who gives her name and invites me, dares me, to show myself, is not a new kind. No. I have been challenged before and will be again. I respond. It is my nature to meet a challenge. I am far more ready than is she. She wants a timid sign, a kiss on the dainty hand, a brief whisper, a distant vision of face and form. I could give her more. She fires up to it. Writhes in frustration. Wants and wants and wants without the end in mind. She would grasp it all, taste and sort and discard and crave crave. She is the most pleasure to me of them all. She thinks I know her and that is true. I found her on a crossroads smelling of her kind. I went for her then. I will go for her again. She pants.*

*Now know that I have many forms and may form more. It is something I can do, like fire, water, flesh.*

*John's mother dared most of all. Anna.*

*My mother, I recall.*

*Anna.*

SATURDAY,
EARLY AFTERNOON,
GREAT ROOM

THE WOMEN

**Sleet weeps down** the windows. The women are seated before the main fireplace, each with a stack of old newspapers. They read silently except for the items they announce to one another.

"I hope these are fake," Melody says. "That's what I hope. I don't see how this many deaths could have happened in one area, and the entire state not take notice. The newspapers have to be some kind of propaganda."

"You're the one who said the local towns publish reproductions." Rachel reaches for the paper Melody holds. "The items do sound like something for a special group like Partners in Crime, or Mysteries Anonymous, or Homicide Revisited." She reads the article to herself. "I see what you mean."

"She was drawn and quartered," Melody responds.

"Or, as the article reports, tortured in a method resembling same."

"Was it in this house?" Connie asks.

"No. In a field off the highway to Sedalia. She was Wilhelmina Mauser. Laundress."

Deborah has evened the sides of her newspaper pile and now places it on the floor next to Rachel. "I'm not reading any of them, thank you. I give up my part in this."

"It was long ago, Deborah."

"I don't care. I'll not read any of them."

Rachel returns to the task, and gradually, except for Deborah, the others do.

"'Charity Smith commits suicide near Sweetwater Creek,'" from Connie. "That's behind this property. November 1873."

"These incidents aren't chronological. Look at the dates. Some are years apart."

"'Five-year-old disappears from back yard.' It's not on this property. In Sedalia, though."

"'Horseback venture turns deadly for young equestrienne.' It's just north of here."

"'Sweetwater Creek claims another victim: Wanda Mecham, missing since December past, found drowned in runoff basin. The young woman's dress was snagged on a submerged log.'"

"This one happened right here," Shelley says. "In this very room."

> *John Belford, son of Mr. and Mrs. William Belford, was seriously injured in a fall at home, known locally as the Sweetwater Music Academy for Ladies. The young man, seventeen, fell from an upstairs banister to the main floor. He sustained several broken bones, including both legs.*

"That explains the canes," Rachel says. "There are canes in the boy's room upstairs."

"If that newspaper article's real, the others are, too," from Deborah.

"Not necessarily. Probably there's just one factual piece here and there. We'd have to verify everything elsewhere."

"Here's another one," Connie rattles the paper. "A woman was killed with hatpins."

"That has to be phony. Hatpins aren't sturdy enough." Deborah.

"There's a hat tree upstairs," Rachel reminds her, "with hats and hatpins."

"Why must you do that?"

"Sorry, Deb."

"Pass me the paper about the boy falling," Connie says.

The window on the landing is sliced with freezing rain. Sleet slides slower down the other windows, congregates at the bottom. There is no wind. Rachel goes for a log, puts it on top of the others. Sparks shoot up and out, die.

"Even if we get iced in, we wouldn't be stuck here," Deborah says, her voice a little querulous. "Our husbands would come for us. There's not a chance they would leave us alone if a real monster storm settles in, is there? Mine will come after me if he can't reach me by phone. He fills the car up for me, puts a bag of kitty litter in the car so I can use it on icy sidewalks. He's a gentleman."

"Ben would probably wait to hear from me," Melody says, "especially since there's a group of us. We're supposed to be busy. Now, if we're not home by tomorrow afternoon, he might come."

"What about your husband, Rachel? Would he come looking for you?"

"I don't know. This is a first. He might be glad to be rid of me."

Melody takes the papers from Connie, adds them to her own stack. "I'll put all the papers back in the office, Rachel. You can photograph articles later."

"If they were really authentic, I think your historical society would have grabbed them long ago."

"They're not hasty people. It's hard to store papers

without doing it right. But I agree with you in some ways. I don't think they're real."

"Whether they are or not," Deborah says, "I'm beginning to think we're being *asked* to leave. I wouldn't mind if we did."

"We can't leave," Rachel says. "Look at what we're finding."

Deborah, lips twisted, worries with her cell phone. "Would you all try your phone?" she asks. "I can't get service. We need a phone line, at least that."

Her concern is contagious in varying degrees. Shelley, content there's no connection, does check, to be in accord with the others. No one has a connected line.

"It doesn't change anything, Deb," Rachel says. "Seriously. Except that you're stirring everyone up."

"Not you, obviously," spoken so charmingly, and properly, that Rachel laughs, as does Connie, and then the others. Deborah, too.

# ANNA

**I don't know** where those newspapers came from. I know none of the names except John and William Belford — my son and husband. I recall the names of our students, our friends, our joys. Our great losses. The women need to know what did happen here, who does live here — if living is the word. What do I do? Wait. Wait and dream. Wake, then dream again. Our John watched the girls, the students, as they practiced. I sometimes knew he was behind the wall because the very air strangled the music. He wanted. I told William I think the boy spies on the girls as they come and go. William lay in wait off the back trail and saw that it was true. Our son followed, occasionally stepping into the open as if inviting discovery should the girl happen to turn just then.

"It's like he wants to get caught," William said. "It's a game with him. An ugly game, I admit, but he's not going to hurt anyone. He's young and he's shy. He'll obey me."

Without consulting William, I asked a minister in Sedalia if he could cleanse our house. I knew such cleansing was possible. The Episcopal minister who visited the orphanage where I finished my childhood had blessed homes for a modest fee. He blessed the orphanage, too, often. One Sunday afternoon he blessed all the animals that people brought. I wanted him to bless me specifically, to transmit to me whatever came down to him from heaven, so I would be safe and happy and would live with my mother after my death. With my mother at least. A father, too, if that were possible, a father with whom one could be happy and not hollow with loneliness in long, dark nights.

The Sedalia minister questioned me. "Why do you feel the need for a blessing now? You have lived in the house for some time."

"I want to feel good about my home," I told him. "It was built before the war and was used, I'm afraid, in terrible ways. I would like God's presence to flood it. I would like blessings on my family."

"You have children?"

"One. A son."

"Is he healthy?"

"His body is."

He was troubled for me, I saw, and seeking direction for himself by studying my posture, my intensity. What needs does this woman have?

"He's fifteen," I said. "He's very temperamental and too quiet, as if he's not with me, with us."

"Does he hear voices?"

"I believe he does."

He told me he had known a family back east whose son, a young man, would suddenly disappear from home, and when he returned weeks later would be rail thin and ill. Twice they learned he had been in a nearby town, working frantically at anything he found, chopping wood, harrowing, breaking horses. He slept only minutes at a time, and he ate hurriedly so he could return to labor. Once he joined a passing carnival and the parents tracked the carnival down and brought him home.

"It's a medical condition and not, I understand, treatable. He would work away the madness. Your son may suffer from a similar malady."

"That might be a blessing," I said. "I believe it's more than a malady."

"You're not an Episcopalian, are you? I've never seen you in service."

"I love God. I don't believe in any one creed."

"I see." He toyed with a Bible on the desk, caressing the leather top. "You might get more comfort if you would talk with the Catholic priest. You would like him. He's young and," he smiled, "a bit lazy. But he's very easy to talk with. Are you averse to Catholicism?"

"I'm not averse to any form of Christianity except those that punish unbelievers."

"We agree there," he said. In moments he had walked me outside, into a lovely day. "If he doesn't want to do the blessing, or some other ritual for you, you can come here again. I would be happy to talk with you."

He was kind.

I went immediately to the priest. There is a somberness and grandeur in the poorest of Catholic churches, or so I believe. I fear they house the old god, the real one, the one to whom I pray, although I pray a little slant always, fearing that he has never approved of me. Still, I will approve of him.

The priest was very young. I felt foolish appealing to him, but he was the hope offered. "There's a heaviness in our home," I said, "a foreboding. The house may have been used during the war for some violent acts. The cellar suggests so. And there's an extensive passage, places to hide. A cemetery is behind the house. I find myself thinking of death. This pall has affected our son. He enjoys the passage. And solitude. He talks to himself or seems to."

"Are you asking me to perform an exorcism?"

I felt exposed, though of course I had been seeking his true understanding. And seeking help. The stating aloud of the word made it seem accurate. The only word. The only ritual.

"I don't know. That would come from your knowledge more than mine. I believe a blessing could do only good, and that is what I seek. The bestowal of good throughout our home."

He studied me, not quite as kindly as had the minister. They have to separate the sane from the insane, the human from the demonic. They have to gauge the nature of the witness, of the petition, and even of a miracle. Not all is as it appears.

"Would you visit my home and talk with my son? Judge the situation yourself?"

"Would your husband be home?"

"No. I assure you our son will be."

He nodded thoughtfully, obviously wondering at my nature. He suddenly decided. "I'll come. I want to help however I can. Friday, about 2:00 in the afternoon?"

When the priest arrived that Friday, he tied his horse to the fence in back, begged a water bucket from me.

He and John strolled around the grounds and then entered the house. John ran upstairs and brought down his sketches. He and the priest sat before the south window, at the small oak table.

"I write poetry," the priest said. "Not too good, very likely. I write from my beliefs and to them, sometimes convincing myself."

"I do the same," John said. "I draw what I see and want to see."

John's drawings were gentle and lovely, just tiny

things in the natural world, identifiable. Precious. My relief was unfathomable. The priest and my son were compatible.

The priest raised his brows at me and smiled. It was a gift. He found no trouble here. He asked to be shown the passage he had heard about. John took him into the music room. I assumed that was so they need not open the panel near me. I couldn't hear them moving in the passage, but I did hear when they went down the stairs to the cellar, and shortly saw them in the side yard. The priest looked beseechingly at the house. I went out and he came to me eagerly. John had walked away, to the fence and over it, toward the woods. He stopped at midfield and turned, watching us. The afternoon sun illuminated his outline, obscured his features. He was half light, half dark. I wondered if he planned that, young boy that he was.

"I do think there's a problem here, with your son," the priest said. "When we were in the passage, he wouldn't speak, even when I asked him to. His bearing seemed different. He seemed heavier and taller. That may be because I was more than a little uneasy at being in a confined space, a dark space. That was itself a struggle. There was a distinct difference, though. He was a threat to me." He stopped, assessed my reaction. "I assume this is why you came to me."

"Yes."

"At this moment, it's tempting to believe that the

situation engaged my imagination, yet in deference to your honesty and concern," here he glanced back at the field where John stood watching us, "I believe there is a danger in this place. He was very different. He was not the young man I sat at table with." He looked at John again. "He still isn't. I am actually afraid to ride home, and to leave you here. I believe you should be afraid, too. When is your husband due? I could stay."

"He won't hurt me. Will you help us?"

"I'm afraid to. I might die trying. There are priests trained to do . . . difficult rituals, and who have an invincible faith."

"Couldn't you do a simple ritual? Could you sprinkle holy water throughout the house? I have heard that could put our house at peace."

Again, he considered. He didn't seem cowardly, merely self-aware, and honest. "I'd probably make it worse, which I think has happened today, and we wouldn't want that. I can give you holy water if you wish to sprinkle it yourself." He met my eyes. "The Lord's Prayer repeated is the simplest ritual. That and the water might be the best remedy, especially delivered with the strength of your faith. Unless you feel in danger."

"It's my son I fear for."

"I can see why. That fate is already in God's hands." He untied his horse and when it swung its head toward the bucket, he pulled it back.

When he mounted the horse, he said, "I'll think this over, and try to find help for you."

"I'll come for the holy water."

"Good. That would be better than my bringing it here, which he would no doubt see."

He rode off, and I listened to the sound of the horse's hooves on the gravel. I was listening for the priest's safety. When I entered the house, John was in the great room.

"I doubt his poetry has much substance, since he himself has little."

That was John, before Elizabeth and the others. Many may have preceded our presence on the land.

Evil had taken abode in my house and then in my son. Intelligent. Cunning. And perhaps angry — born angry or turned that way.

What horror would it be to suspect that you were the evil? Did my son sometimes know? Did he lament what he was and beg for rescue? I would. I would scream for help. If silenced, then what? Torment.

He's here. He smiles at me from the kitchen door and bows his head. His dark hair falls around his cheeks and when he straightens, he is exactly my son, and I gasp at the pain of it.

I did visit the priest and ask for holy water. I remember the lighted candles alongside the sanctuary. Petitions to the highest power. I had made many in prayers. The priest gave me a small, corked bottle. At home again, I put a drop of the blessed water on my tongue. I went up the stairs to my son's room and entered without knocking. "What do you have there?" he asked, and I told him the truth. "Holy water from the Church." He watched me uncork the bottle. I held it firm lest he strike it away. He was at his desk and he turned his face up as if offering himself. I think that was John, my son. I wiped a small amount across his forehead and touched his closed eyelids with a moistened finger. The eyes remained closed. When I had corked the bottle and stood near the door, I said, "John?" The eyes opened, soft, then hard, flat. "There's nothing wrong with me, Mother," he said, "but there's something terribly wrong with you. Leave us alone."

Didn't I catch his word, the word meant to advise me who was speaking. "Us," he had said. "Leave us alone."

Still, I doubted myself. What was this? What was he?

Did a devil really walk the earth, I asked William. Really? Or was it a force, just like a wind or an illness, that touched people. A natural evil?

"A devil," William said. "No matter what you call it, Anna, it's a devil. If you would believe in a being who cares for us all and in whose grace we are safe, then you must believe in his enemy, a mighty foe. And beautiful, they say." He kissed my forehead. "There's the danger."

I had no power strong enough to help John then and none to help him now. How to help even these women? Stay by them. Go with them as I have gone with John. Learn what I can. Do what I can.

# SATURDAY, MIDAFTERNOON

## JOHN

**My ladies.**

*If I could touch them all at one time, I would. It is almost possible. I can grasp the concept and can almost effect it. I love touch, all kinds. The finger to bark, the slip into water, the veining of leaves, the lacing of blood. I can sometimes, not often enough, immerse into and fill to brimming another. It won't sustain. For me, it is a deep breath of full life, senses, smells, tastes, past and present, a little being totally mine. Then gone. That is the nature of everything. Piece here, piece there, so rarely the whole. This place is mine. This hill and waterway, and deep springs, and caverns. Mine. I have branched afar, but not far enough. I want to net under the surface, meet myself, and close in everything within. This is my knowledge, my nature. Men want to sing the universe, ring the planets. They have a grand idea of the journeys they are gifted. Crawling is not in their scheme. It is what they do.*

*Anna wanted to see me and she saw me, and will see me again. Here, sweet. Here sughy.*

*John liked touch. He liked all senses. He burned with want. He was a guileless little creature, for a long time. John, I would whisper. John, think on this. Observe her. And that one. And that one. Think on this. Ha!*

*I can bite the head from an eagle. Cut the breasts from a girl.*

*John's mother thought she had me. She crept from the hallway upstairs, rushed and cried out at the same time and swung a heavy lantern at her boy's neck. It caught him just so and he tumbled over the railing, landing on his back, legs askew, staring up at his mother. "I didn't do anything," he moaned. "I didn't do it."*

*She thought to thwart me. She didn't understand. I could act with him or without him. I could make his broken body strain for perfect stance. I can act without anyone. I do enjoy companionship. The burst of freshness. I am fond of all creation, myself included. I didn't make me. I don't know what I am. I've had no choice.*

# SATURDAY,
# MIDAFTERNOON
# MELODY'S STORY

**Melody angles the** cane back chair by the fireplace, places a paper napkin down on the stone skirt, and sets her coffee cup there. It's from the house's cupboard, a white, heavy one common in restaurants. She's always liked that kind of cup, nothing pretentious about it. The vastness of the room and the meager lighting distorts the faces before her, but, because of the woman upstairs she allows herself a slow beginning, seeking to identify every position, every shape now. While she dislikes not disclosing fully what she and two others have uncovered, she wants, as does Rachel, the magic and gravity of discovery, of being first, of making the record. She is an honest person, though, and will eventually have to share all.

"My grandmother could see ghosts," Melody begins, "not in photos, as many people can do, but always at funerals and wakes, and also in other places. She said they often appeared as 'one more.' She would see six people, say, on a bench, or five in line at the casket, and a second later she would see a different number. She learned to see a group first, as a whole backdrop, and then search for individuals. A face might be missing. Scoffers explain it away as a misreading of space — a viewer sees an empty space between two parties as a third party. But the extra guests I'm speaking of aren't vague. They have distinguishing features, a bonnet, or lantern jaw, or a mole, and appear to know they've been caught. Maybe they want to be.

"As for me, I believe I've seen ghosts, not often and not all that may be around. I don't understand what causes it to occur. When I was seven, my brother, who was five, was playing in a shallow part of Post Oak, while I sat on a tree root that curved out high from the bank. I was above him and could see the tops of the banks and down the river. My brother had a pole and line with a safety-pin for a hook. He squealed, and I thought he had something. He had gotten in over his head. I scrambled up, ready to jump, when I saw he wasn't alone. In the water with him were a man and woman. I hadn't seen them seconds before, though the banks lay straight, no deep bends and no heavy shrubbery. Where had they come from? The man, in the deeper water, pushed my brother toward the woman, who pulled him into her arms and carried him a few feet to the bank. I didn't get down, because while it happened fast, it seemed slow, unreal, and too quiet. It was like two times simultaneously, and I was in both, or privy to both. The man emerged, the woman brushed the hair from my brother's face, and turned around as if she had known all along right where I was. No searching for me. I wondered if they had been watching us earlier. She had light blue eyes, white-blond hair, and was very, very thin. The couple climbed up the bank, sort of angling the other direction. I didn't take my eyes off them. I expected them to disappear. In one blink, they were gone, as suddenly as they had come. They didn't walk away. They didn't go down toward the water. They should have been visible and audible. They weren't.

"My brother and I told my mom and dad and Granny, too. My mom said the couple were angels, and Granny said they were ghosts, probably a couple who drowned or lost a child to drowning. My dad wouldn't give his opinion.

"That's not my ghost story, though. It's my introduction. I believe everybody sees ghosts. They may not admit to it or not know it until later, as I didn't."

"Same is true of angels," Connie says. "You can't be certain which one you're talking about."

"Maybe you can. Maybe there's a test we haven't learned." The chair arms are the perfect length for Melody, and her fingers fit into the grooved ends. This pleases her.

It's a nice, quality chair. She would like to own a few pieces like this, a desire that conflicts with her principles. She wants to serve. "Here's the story I came to share, the one that puzzles me.

"Every October, the Mason Genealogical Society sponsors a Cemetery Walk as a fundraiser. I imagine some of you know about it. It's been an annual event for fifteen years. Volunteers from campus and town dress in period costumes and assume the roles of distinguished deceased persons from our community. The actors stay within a few feet of the appropriate grave and when a small group has gathered, the actors go into the routine, taking on the persona of the character, speaking in the first person about accomplishments, and trials and tribulations. They tell who they are, what they're noted for—the script varies every now and then when someone adds facts from research. A few of the actors are quite good. I've been a ghost several times. I like to do it right and always research my character. I make my costume instead of borrowing from the historical society. It's authentic, too—the cloth, threads, buttons. I have a whole wardrobe. If I were a true actress, which, unfortunately, I'm not, I could dress for any part. While I can make the costumes, I can't disguise my nature.

"Two years ago, I chose to tour rather than participate as a ghost. I got into a carriage, an elegant one, restored, that had actually been used in funeral processions at the turn of the century. I boarded it at the gatehouse and, along with three other people, rode up the first hill. It was midafternoon, October. It was a golden day, with the sun thick and heavy over the little hills. The sun struck from the west at that time of day, and since graves lie, as you may know, with headstones facing the sunrise, shadows fell over the graves. It was almost like the night covered them again, in patches. And throughout the cemetery actors played their parts.

"The carriage couldn't come close to all the actors, only those near the road. I could see a man near a northeast section plot, where two students who died in the university fire in 1915 are buried, a young girl and a young man. The boy's father was so grieved that he left funds to purchase plots for any student who ever perished here from whatever cause and whose family could not afford burial. Usually, a young girl played a role there, too. I wanted to know the new actor's name, if he volunteered from genealogy or the historical society, or one of the city repertory groups. I couldn't place him. I descended from the carriage and crossed the grassy lawn—there were no formal paths. He saw me coming and doffed his hat in that way some men have, keeping the crown up and the lining toward the ground, as if it's too crude or too intimate for a lady to see, and he bowed a little even before I reached him.

"'Welcome, Miss,' he said. 'Thank you for being

interested in my story.' He was looking directly at me then. His eyes were pretty, the expression soft as if he were nearsighted, and he had a pleasant, deep voice. I liked him. He was a dandy in dress, charming—a brown suit with a yellow scarf, high boots a much lighter color than the suit and very clean.

"'I was caught where the fire started,' he said, 'in Dockery, the top floor. Fire was racing up the stairs and blazing on the roof. It had leapt to the library and a dormitory. Fire and smoke everywhere, like a war. I was trapped on the roof, unable to get the three floors down to safety. Agony. You can imagine. I was burned beyond recognition.'

"As he talked, his demeanor changed. He canted his head as if imploring understanding, as if asking, 'Do you see?' and he was peering at me in an odd way. I felt very sorry for him. I also knew there was something behind the words, more than the story of the young man who died. Something painful and dangerous. I told him I didn't think anyone had died in Dockery, only in the dormitory, and that the buried victim's father hadn't believed for a long time that his son was dead, because he wasn't supposed to be in the dormitory.

"'Others were missing, too,' he said, 'that were never found. To this day, I am positive. Not found.'

"I felt he was flirting with me, which seemed

inappropriate given the topic."

"He *was* toying with you," Connie says. "That's what you felt was inappropriate. A game he was playing without your knowledge. He was making an ugly, painful subject intimate and exciting. It's what some witches do and can give them away."

"I know. I told him I needed to go, and he should, too. The tour was over, the carriage had made the loop and was at the gatehouse. The other strollers were almost down the hill. He and I were alone, with him smiling that way, as if we were in on something together. Leaves swirled around us, sounded like so many whispers. I wanted to escape but wouldn't turn my back to him. I sort of edged away, and he laughed, made a half lunge at me, teasing. He looked down the hill at the others, then at me. Something had shifted. He quietened. His eyes stopped smiling. I remembered then the name of the boy who died. It was on the headstone, too, which he was blocking.

"'What's your name,' I asked him.

"'Will.'

"'Will what?'

"'Will. That'll do. I'm one they didn't find.'

"I retreated, keeping him in view, until he just wasn't there. I ran down the hill toward the others, and for a minute I felt more terrified because I suddenly realized maybe none of them was real. The sun was slanting down the road like the end of day was the next second or two and the road would be black, and I'd be there alone."

She frowns, looks aside for a moment, then resumes. "I thought he started the fire or enjoyed it some way. Even if he was a victim, too. And he wanted to talk about it, as some people do, who enjoy recalling another's pain, especially if they caused it." She adjusts her position in the chair. She sips from the coffee cup.

"You've scared me," Rachel says. "Lord. Who was he?"

"I don't know. We didn't have a volunteer for that character. I looked for records of a Will anybody who was a student in 1915. Those records and the preceding ones were destroyed. I don't even know if his name was Will. What I do know is that he visits the campus, because I saw him there." She raises two fingers. "Twice. He may have been there other times when I didn't see him. I suspect he was."

"Where on campus did you see him?"

"Once in Dockery. That's the building, restored, where the fire started. Or so they think. I had just gotten in the elevator, and after I pushed the button, there he was, outside the elevator, the door closing. I tell you . . . " She has lost her usual composure, her mellow voice wavering. "I thought I'd burn up for sure, in the elevator, you know? I thought he was reminding me of fire to scare me.

"That's the story I wanted to tell. I can see ghosts. And they can see me. I don't know if it's something I do or is from the timing or situation. I know this wasn't a nice young man. If some ghosts like to do harm, I suspect this was one of them."

"You're right about that," Connie says. "There are bound to be mean ones. Ghosts are a species, aren't they? At least a part of the human species, as Rachel says. Most species have individual types, and certainly humans do. Some deranged people are kind natured, others vicious and wicked. Maybe even a disease has its own personality. The afterlife is probably governed by the same rules as this life. A basic self, a diseased self, a blessed self, a damned self. An ancient self."

"I give up," Rachel mumbles. "You *want* a damnation to be possible. Damnation is not a personality type. Neither is blessed."

"I might quarrel with you there if you allowed it. However, research does show there's something after death, and a personality is one of the possibilities they name. Maybe it's the force of a personality."

"That's a lot like picking up a mindset, isn't it?" Rachel observes. "These floating possibilities that we can just suddenly house."

"I'm not saying that. It's not that definite. But why not, Rachel? The natural world has creatures controlling others—parasites changing the nature and action of another species. We don't know what we're carrying every minute or what's waiting to be hosted—what power they might have over us."

"Stop it, Connie. Okay? Back to ghosts and stories."

"All right. I'll stop. I do want us to talk about this stuff eventually, before we're finished here."

"You saw him again, Melody?" Shelley asks.

"In the library. I was in the stacks, and he was suddenly there, with that same amused expression, like he was coaxing the intended." Her gaze drifts from Shelley's face to the other women and to the rim of their circle's light. She expects the fellow to be here because she mentioned him. She's not afraid of him so much as ignorant of how to handle him.

"Why would he appear to you again somewhere else?" Deborah asks. "Doesn't he have to have a place he haunts? Can a ghost *stalk*? I saw my ghost—the ghost I saw—only once and in one place. He stayed there. He has to, doesn't he?"

"Maybe ghosts are free to travel the paths of their life," Connie says. "Even further. If they're learning and interacting, even evolving."

"Stop that." Deborah gestures to the windows. "*This* is evolving. In a few hours we may have trouble getting out, and we don't know anything about this place. The whole roof may cave in. The heating may not work. We're miles away from help."

"We have two fireplaces down here, Deborah, and that heat will help the upstairs. If it freezes over, which I admit it's likely to do, we're better off here than on the road."

"Not true," Deborah says. "An hour on the road and we're home. Twelve hours here and we're still here and an hour *away* from home. I probably wanted this weekend more than any of you did, but it's not what I expected. I feel in jeopardy. I've never been this nervous. Things aren't likely to get better now, are they? And I'm ill, whether from allergies, chemicals, even ghosts—whatever—I'm convinced we need to get out of here. I'm surer than I've ever been about anything. I wish you'd trust me."

"We can all go," Shelley suggests earnestly. "We don't have to spend the night. But I would like to tell my ghost story first. I can tell mine and then Connie can tell hers. We have time. We can be off the premises by eight p.m. at the very latest. If we leave now, only half of us got to participate and the other half were just listeners. I want to tell my story. It's the fair thing to do. Isn't it?" She directs the question to Connie.

"Yes, it is. It's a good way to slow down, too, and make rational decisions."

"I'm rational," Deborah states. "Completely rational. Yes, I'm afraid—it feels absolutely right to be. I'm afraid for all of us."

Something clatters over the roof.

"That was too heavy for sleet," Connie says. "Branches are breaking off. The trees are freezing."

"We're not trapped here, Deborah," Rachel says, soothingly. "We can get out of here if we want, We're not in need. We're in a comfortable house, our husbands know where we are, and we have each other. Nothing has happened that has harmed or even threatened any of us. We're hoping for at least a sign."

"I'm going to check the car."

"Don't take off, Deborah. Don't do that."

"I won't. I promise. Don't worry. I'll warm the motor up. Make sure it's working. That's all." She's already wearing her coat, disappearing toward the mudroom.

They wait. The silence lasts too long, then comes the motor roar, the decrease into drive, and again quiet. Rachel says, "She's coming back."

In seconds, Deborah enters the great room. Her upper coat is almost black from sleet.

"I moved the car so it's pointed downhill," she says, ruddy-cheeked and proud. "I saw a truck on the highway. It means someone can get around. I guess I can wait a while. Even longer if I must."

It is midafternoon but night-like. The fire hisses and crackles.

"Okay, girls," Rachel says, "let's get back on track. We'll plan on being out by eight. That gives us time to investigate a little more, get some photos, hear Shelley's story at say six, Connie's at seven, and head for home at eight. Even with slow travel, we'll be home by ten. How's that? We can and will leave at eight unless we *choose*—all of us, Deborah, all of us—*choose* to stay, with a fire in each fireplace, camaraderie, the ice storm sealing a wonderful story. This is exactly what we wanted, I thought, a little excitement. You all know I want to stay. I'm conceding, though it hurts."

# ANNA

**I remember ice** and cold, and the house itself chilly everywhere away from the fire. With life there, William, John, and hope, the chill was temporary, remediable. Now, I doubt what is and can be. Can the women leave safely without me? With me? I wish William would come now, embrace me, tell me, "Anna girl, this is what we'll do."

I speak aloud for whatever listens. "I will stay here."

The girls loved to tease our boy. When I saw the other peering from his eyes, I said, "You must never harm anyone, not anyone. None of the girls."

"'I only look," he said.

"You must stop even that." He wanted me to know. That was part of his nature. Is part.

I arranged for my students who had to walk here to travel in pairs, no matter which direction they came from. Even if they had only to walk down the slope to the road below, they were never to be alone. They made their own plans, as girls do.

One was ever sweet to him. Elizabeth. She was a

valentine herself, small, white-blond hair in loose curls, blue eyes, and nice ways. A kind girl. Full of questions and delight. "Quiet John," she called him. I heard her ask him to play violin for her. "I know you play. I imagine it's most beautiful." Another time she said, "John, have you heard of serenading? A beau stands in the moonlight and plays love songs beneath his sweetheart's window." She was fond of him.

Elizabeth was found hanging from a branch of a sycamore tree. The body was close to the tree trunk and on the side facing the path. Her father found her. It brought him to his knees, I heard, when he looked up — by chance or because the heart knows — and saw a form almost invisible against the mottled bark.

She was a tiny thing. She could sing. Her laughter was a pure, clear sound, like water in glass. Her violin was gone, the bow and case, too. They found the strings wrapped like bracelets around her wrists. Found other wounds.

Three men from town came, one of them the sheriff. They had William come outside first. I watched from the house. They seemed so slow and big. Many nods and knowing glances, being powerful and in control. My son so slight among them. They didn't call for me. I wanted them to. I strode out, determined to hear what they had to say and to say my own piece. Don't question us separately. Don't say it in dollops. Say it straight, right at us. They waved me back in. William came and took my elbow and said, "Anna, stay out of this. It's more than anyone should have to hear."

They had asked John to wait, and he sat on a fence post, that small cemetery close behind him. He was balanced so his heels caught on the lower rail and he worked the rail back and forth as he watched the men, curious, not anxious. I studied him. With his name and a come-here gesture they called him over, and he hopped down obediently and stood by them. The sheriff said something to him and John held his hands out. The sheriff examined them, front and back. He slipped the shirt cuffs up and checked wrists and forearms. Then he turned John's face from side to side. The men shielded him from my view and I knew they searched for scratches on his legs and torso. When they parted again, John was the same as before. Polite and quiet. They motioned him toward the house and I ran inside. He came through the great room, tramped past me and up to his room.

William came in. "They said he couldn't have done it. He's not strong enough to have put her where they found her. And there's not a mark on him. I thought for a few minutes they were going to examine me. They still may."

We talked in whispers about Elizabeth and her parents. The whole community. What had passed among us.

"He had to be immensely strong and like an animal,

some crazed fellow who jumped from the railroad and has gone on." William squeezed his eyes shut for a few seconds. "Lord, let that be the case. Passing through and long gone." He shook those thoughts away. "I'm proud of John. He followed their instructions without complaint, though they offered no explanation."

"He didn't ask?"

"He was scared. He had to be. Sick from it, probably. I am. I'll talk with him now."

He left. I hurried to the kitchen, into the pantry, and down into the cellar. I thought something might draw me to it as water draws the dowsing rod and the dowser, thought I might smell blood or fear. Part of the floor was dirt and I scanned for a spot newly disturbed, for a piece of wire or cloth or ribbon. Hair. I searched in the bins of vegetables, among William's tools, canning jars, boxes. I peered in the crannies of the wood stack.

Images assail a woman at such times. A story becomes images and the images hide in the mind.

I said a prayer for her, the same one over and over. I couldn't break away from the happening itself, the horror of it. As if it had flowed into me like poison.

I returned upstairs and began the common busyness of duties. I peeled potatoes and diced them and sliced onions into them and dropped them into a skillet of sizzling lard. I stirred them, poured a little water into the pan, and capped the lid on it, to let them soften and then brown as the water evaporated. I salted water and leached the liver until the flesh had turned gray. I had been taught that bloody meat carried diseases and bad vapors. I dredged the pieces in flour and fried them quickly to set the flour and seal the meat, then let them cook slowly till done.

Think on the sparrow, on the lilies.

My husband and son came down together, sat at the dining table. I carried in blue plates, tableware, a bowl of cucumbers and onions and tomatoes soaked in vinegar and sugar. I brought in the sturdy food close together, meat, potatoes, cornbread, corn, and a lemon cake which my mother favored. William said a blessing.

William made an effort to eat, then ceased even the pretense. I feared John would have his normal appetite, sealing my suspicions. Instead, he followed his father's gesture, and shoved his plate away. He turned his face to me and I saw my John, his silent raw need — *Save me. Help me.* I won't let myself forget that. We never know what scenes play in another's mind, what their reality is in the midst of our own. What cry they would make if they could.

These women do not know my son or his usurper. He can't make any new thing, but he can mimic what he will. That must be true. He can whisper a truth and impart a lie or whisper a lie and impart a truth. He conjectures and guides a mind where it should not go.

"Before we do anything else," Melody says, "we eat. We're running on nerves now."

Rachel kneels by the sandalwood box she brought from my son's room. "Let's go through this stuff next." She drags the box toward the fireplace near which they tell their stories, and then stretches and rubs the back of her neck. "I wish we had more flashlights. And time. There's not enough time to do everything right."

"We've got plenty of candles and a few kerosene lamps," Melody says. "They'll do, if we need them."

"I wouldn't want to use either one in the passage."

"You don't need to go in there again," from Shelley.

"Yes, I do. We need evidence we can keep."

"Evidence of what?" Deborah.

"Anything we see, hon. A door. A hole in the wall. The passage itself."

In a moment, Deborah nods as if she knows exactly what is not being said. "Okay."

If the contents of the box belong to my son, they are mine. His story is not to be bruited about, not without my consent. I'm his protector, as much as I am theirs. If I could steal the box away and bury it forever, I would do so. I want to save his soul from condemnation. I want to trade my own.

# THE WOMEN

**They sit in** a circle on the floor before the fireplace, with Rachel presiding over the box from the small bedroom. Candles reflect against the iced windows, as if a group of ghost women watch from the other side.

"He was a little botanist," Melody says. "These drawings are really good."

"He could carve, too. If this is his."

From the box, they take music miscellany—strings, rosin, bridges.

"What's this?" Rachel holds up a peg of wood. Connie takes it.

"A soundpost. Fits in a fiddle."

Rachel holds a sheet of drawing paper. "My God. Whoever drew this is sick. Was sick." Her hand trembles. She transfers the sketch to Connie, takes out another.

No one wants to hold them. Shelley, last, lays each face-down on the floor. Connie gathers them.

"We'll take them to the police," Rachel says, "as soon as we're home. Whether or not they're real. We'll take them with us. I promise they'll go to the authorities."

"Are you honestly willing to give them up?" Connie asks. "Honestly?"

Rachel bites her lip. "I'll copy them first."

"Listen to what's on the back. 'Ruth Campbell, 1933.'" Connie turns over another, "'Dorothy Lamson, 1937.'" Another, "'Vera Cambrey, 1938.'" The last, "'Harriet Wray, 1943.'"

"May he be long dead," Melody says.

Rachel lifts a packet of butcher paper from the bottom of the box, begins unfolding it. Melody kneels to help her extend it on the floor, like a strip of land between them.

"It's a timeline. Starts in the 1870s."

"It's a map."

Dates, buildings, roads, towns. Stick figures are here and there, made female with feathery strokes for hair and half-curls for breasts. The women look at one another.

Melody sits back on her heels and holds the paper by the two corners, stretching it enough to flatten the creases. "These are victims. This is the personal timeline of a murderer. That's why it was in the box. It goes along with those sketches. It's a murderer's record."

"Someone interested in murders, more likely," Rachel says. "It covers too many years to be the history of one person."

"It could be a family of killers," Connie says, "and they pass the record on. But the penwork does look like one person did it, same figures and lettering. Whoever did it, one or many, wanted someone to see it, wanted people to know what had been done."

"Right." Melody nods. "Right. That's pretty scary. Someone has to stop it."

"Don't worry," Rachel says. "It can't be real. We couldn't be the first to find it. There are other things here . . . Everything is probably planted."

"Then let's go home," from Deborah.

"No. It's still a story."

"Then burn the paper."

"No way," Rachel blurts. "No. Absolutely not. If this all ties together with the dates in the paper, we need it. It's the best part yet. Even if it's planted. We're keeping it. It's evidence of our experience and I'm not giving it up."

Melody jerks the paper but Rachel holds fast. The long strip rips in two. Melody crushes her piece together and casts it on the flames.

"Good for you, Melody," Deborah says. "Good. Burn the rest of it, too."

Rachel has saved the remainder. She pulls it to herself, folds it back as it was folded. "We're supposed to plan together."

"We're already acting separately, aren't we? You are, Rachel," from Connie, her glance including Shelley and Melody.

"If he meant the blank part for more victims," Melody says, "that plan's dead. Thank God."

# ANNA

**He could have** committed those horrors through hands other than his own. Years don't stop him. Or if they do, I'm too limited to know. Where he began, where he ends. The stories could be lies, too. He could tell them to inflict fear and pain. And haste. Hatred. I know him. He didn't divulge his nature to me. I discovered it, and each little knowing was another defeat and another desire. I wanted to be the death of him, not the death of John.

Weeks I searched for evidence. Weeks after the men left our property, weeks after Elizabeth had been buried by her family, and I and William and John had stood with others in the church cemetery. Weeks during which I expected something to cry out to me, here, here is the proof of your suspicion. Inside, outside, in cupboards, in the yard, drawers, wagon, shelves. Then, as I stood at my bedroom window, I saw a small round spoke of wood at the lower right joint of the frame. I knew what it was. I opened the window, clenched the object. My mouth went dry and nausea brought me to sit on the bed. I felt as if

God himself watched me, toyed with me. I examined the piece in the lamp light. A few miniscule scratches where a musician's tool might have repositioned it. Not naturally this smooth. The soundpost of a violin, outside my window. My window. I waited, sick, for William to come up. He always came last, securing the house for us. I intended to show him. I didn't, because it had been outside our window, not John's. It was where someone in the room might think on it, know about it, might raise the window to touch it. Might. I put it in my pillowcase and shook it down as I fluffed the pillow.

"You should see yourself in the moonlight," William said. "Lovely woman."

He came to kiss me, and to lie with me. When he raised his body over mine, I thought of what rage in a man that strong might be. How a small woman had no chance at survival if a man like William wanted to hurt her. So fragile! Begging would be her only recourse. I tried to think of Elizabeth realizing what the man intended, what he was. I was willing to know the truth. Could I fear him? Could I? No. He was comfort. A good man. All my instincts said so. All my love. A good man. I had a choice, to believe he had put the soundpost there, or to believe it had come there another way. I chose.

I showed him the soundpost. He rolled it in his palm, said, "Outside our window? The wind could have done it.

A bird. Why would John do it? Why would he put it on our windowsill? It doesn't make sense."

He wondered if I was lying, if I was building a case against our son, if I was following a fancy too far. If I had put the soundpost there myself, if it had ever been on the sill at all.

"It was a small sign he was giving us. He wants us to know, William. Maybe it's to cause us pain, so we'll stop him."

"Even if he did it," William said, "he's our son. We'll watch him. If we have any indication that he's going to . . . do harm to anyone, we'll take him to St. Louis or back east. There are hospitals. We'll find a place for him. We'll take care of him."

"We may not know what he's doing or will do. We didn't know about Elizabeth."

"Anyone could have done that, Anna. Some crazed soul. The war made crazy people crazier. So many people were being killed the world smelled like blood. I don't believe our boy hurt that girl." He returned the soundpost to me. "We're doing the best we can."

"Most people do," I told him. "I love our son as much as you do. I don't want to hate him. I don't want to spy on him. I don't want to rip him out of your heart. I don't want you to stop loving me because of him."

"I won't. I'll never stop loving you."

I must believe that's true.

I planned to burn the piece of evidence. Instead, I put it in the back of a kitchen drawer, in a lidless box for odds and ends that fit nowhere, a small tin for matches, a little wax for the drawers and windows.

I was willing, anxious, to be wrong. At times John could laugh, tease, transform the day with his youth and maleness. He was often a willing worker, both around this isolated place and at the store in town. He was quick and polite with others. He would wink at me, as William did. He said "Mother" in the sweetest manner, whether question or answer. Or could say it that way. He wrapped packages deftly, tied fancy knots that drew comments from customers. He liked to make rounds to the other stores, and to have a cool drink at the Station Inn.

Then a girl was found on the edge of the field beyond a house for women who did the oldest work. An alley ran behind it, and two doors led to its interior. I don't know what lay inside the doors. I imagine that one allowed access to the front of the house, and the other allowed exit. Our store was the entire main street away from the place. In early November they found the girl, on a Sunday morning, after a dance the night before. We had been at the dance, the three of us. John had danced with me for one of the squares, then had gone outside. The moon was white and high that night. I remember seeing it from the schoolhouse where we danced. A hopeful moon. Romantic moon.

William told me about the girl when he and John came home on Monday evening. John said, "You're going to believe I did it. No doubt." He was seventeen then, holding a cap like the young schoolboy self he was leaving behind. He gestured toward his father. "Why don't you think it was him?"

"Why would I believe it was either of you?"

"You want to believe it. You want to be first to know."

We were in the kitchen. He went into the great room and I heard him at the far fireplace.

I questioned William with my eyes.

"Are you asking me if I did it? My God, no."

I hated to say what I thought. "Did you hear him say one word of denial? Did he say he didn't do it? No. It's his arrogance. He did it."

We stood in silence that had deepened. Both of us, surely, aware of our son. I knew that in the other room, John listened. John heard, even if our words weren't audible. I went in there. He was on one knee before the fire. He tossed something dark and flimsy into the flame, and it was snatched and gone.

"What did you throw in the fire?" I asked.

"Part of a dress, of course," he said. "I just waited for you to see me do it."

William was in the room now. He had heard. "Don't tease your mother."

"She enjoys it." He removed his coat, carrying it toward the rear entry where he and William hung their work coats. "She'll go through my pockets. She may go through yours."

I felt myself a fool, or crazy, ashamed. I thought that the evil was in me, not in my son, in my heart and thoughts, and my son and husband had to protect themselves against me. I embraced this ugliness about myself. I was sick with it. I did want to go through his pockets. And I wanted to examine my son's body. I wanted to slap his cheeks and bring some true fire into those dark eyes that were watching me. Oh, those eyes. They can't hide, some creatures. They must peek out, reveal themselves.

"I'm sorry," I said, meant only for William.

"Don't worry," he said, and held me. "Fear changes everyone." He released me. A few moments later he confronted our son. "John, tell us you didn't do it."

"I didn't do it," said without anguish or even anger. He walked away from us. He didn't stalk away in indignation. He didn't fling up his arms in despair. I thought he was going to his room, but he passed the staircase and went into the music room. We heard a tune. He was playing the violin.

"Do you recognize that tune?" I asked.

"No."

"It's 'Rose Tree.'"

"Is that important?"

"It's what we danced to when John left the schoolhouse."

William brought his own coat to me, then went for John's. I wouldn't check William's pockets. I didn't have to. In a few seconds he brought to me a tiny piece of something, no larger than his thumb nail. "What's this?"

Fabric. Dark blue. Square. It had been cut evenly, not torn.

"I think it's a piece of cloth from the store," I said. "It was cut straight with scissors. He put it there deliberately."

"Why would he do that?"

"He enjoys making me suspicious and frightened. He doesn't care if the evidence is false or true. He wants the doubt."

"You're twisting facts, Anna. Don't you see? No matter what he does, you'll make it fit your suspicions."

"No. You have it backwards. He makes me suspicious by playing with innocence. By being innocent of some things to cast doubt on me. By pretending to be pretending!"

"Anna. Can you hear what you're doing? He's your son."

"I know." I was too agitated, too miserable, and he hushed me. He would, he assured me, find out what the girl was wearing. He would check the piece of cloth against the fabrics in our shop. He would allay my fears.

The cloth was not from our shop. The murdered girl

had, however, worn blue. The dress had been torn from her.

"William," I said, "if someone could scour the alley and our shop, I swear to you threads would be found that match that piece of cloth and that dress. He trimmed it. The dress had been torn so he trimmed a torn piece to have even edges. He was calm enough to trim it, just to enjoy this twisted play. Give the piece to the sheriff. Tell him where we found it."

He bowed his head.

"Willam, do it. It came from the dress."

"I don't have it."

"Why?"

"I don't know. I had it one moment and then I didn't. Someone came into the store. I was careless, Anna. That's all."

"You threw it away to protect him."

"No."

"Burned it."

"No."

"You never lied to me before, William. Not that I know about."

He sighed, went to sit at the table and stared out the window. I was sorry. I didn't want to lose him, too. I stood behind him and slipped my hands down onto his chest. He clasped my wrists, kissed them. "I've never lied to you," he said. "I'm not lying to you now."

I believed him. His carelessness had lost the fabric. There's no safeguard against human frailty.

Another young woman found a sign in town. The murderer had fashioned a small flag by skewering a patch of blue cloth with a twig and sticking it near the pump behind the school. Here the madman was saying, I cleansed myself of blood. Mark this spot.

I emptied the fuel from one of our storm lanterns and removed the globe from the metal frame. Holding it by the bail, I practiced swinging, which made me stumble, made my neck and right arm ache. I placed it on the bottom shelf of a table near the stair landing. I believed what was in John would flee an injured body. On a morning when William was up early and gone to receive an order at the train station and then to the store, I waited in my bedroom for John to rise, and peeked to watch him approach the staircase. As he reached the lip of steps I darted out, grabbed the lamp by the handle and swung as hard as I could. The base caught him across the shoulders, and his right shoulder caved forward, turning his face toward me as he curved over the railing and fell, not down the stairs as I had intended, but over the railing completely, a long fall, and hit the floor with a heavy, dull thud and a shorter sound that I knew was his head. I thought he would be dead. I had killed him. Not my intent. Just to stop him. To separate them.

"I didn't do anything," he moaned from below. "I didn't do it."

I ran down and knelt by him.

"Must you kill me?" he said, his tone so mournful that no matter what creature spoke the words, they wrenched my heart.

I saddled John's mare, and rode into town, first to the doctor's home and office, and then to William. To the doctor I said my son was injured in a fall and might be dying. To my husband, who took my mare in exchange for the wagon, I said, "I tried to wound him enough to stop him. I may have killed him."

William forgave me. "If you're wrong," he told me, "you've crippled the boy needlessly. You've ruined his life."

John didn't tell anyone what I had done. The doctor said he found abrasions on John's back as if he'd been struck or beaten. Did we know how he received those injuries? Had we beaten him?

"No."

The doctor suggested that John had sustained those abrasions in the fall. Had he fallen on anything?

John lied to the doctor for me. I supposed it was for me. "I leaned over too far," he said. "I was looking for my mother."

He healed quickly. He asked no questions. My act lay so heavy on me I wished I could die. I sat by his bed and poured out my heart to him, my sorrow. My worry. "You're not well, John. You know that. Please. Trust me to see the truth. I'm trying to save you from what has overtaken you. That's why I did it."

"Save me by killing me?" His eyes met mine and for a second anguish bonded us. "That wouldn't be the worst fate," he whispered.

That was truly my son.

Sometimes there was a smile behind his eyes, curling the edge of his lips. I had not one steady fiber in my being. I didn't know what more to do. I had crippled him and crippled my husband's spirit. Whenever I could see one remnant of the sensibility I believed was John's, I would say, "I love you."

"I can't bear looking at him," William said. "I pray we're taking care of him the best we can. Maybe we've succeeded. If you're right about him, I mean, maybe we've succeeded."

"Do you believe that I'm right?"

I hoped that he would doubt me, and better yet, prove me wrong. There are times when one wants, terribly, to be in error.

"Unfortunately, yes."

There we were, loving him, afraid of what he was, what he had done and would do. Here I am still.

# SATURDAY,
# LATE AFTERNOON
## LUKE ESSEX

**The guests at** the old Bledsoe house have occupied Luke's mind since the weather turned fierce. He assumes they arrived. He has considered driving over there in case they're in need. No one has phoned him. There's no emergency. Locked in, he has enjoyed music. His small house is as fine-tuned as a recording studio. His bedroom holds a simple single-bed, a reading floor-lamp beside it, a straight-back chair for a nightstand, and a stack of books — many of them collections of songs. He is often weary, since he is in demand as a carpenter, his perfectionism carrying over into any endeavor. Sometimes when he lies down to rest, his muscles bear the memory of the day's work and they twitch in ghostly carpentry; sometimes they play tunes. Both forms are art to Luke. As is lovemaking. He is not as particular in that area, loving women in general.

He practices "Elzic's Farewell" for an hour, records it;

then "Whippoorwill Reel" for an hour and records it. He puts away his fiddle, turns off his recording equipment, heats a bowl of thin tomato soup, turns up the sound on the radio. Since the house is small, the basement is, too, and with no windows it's cell-like, not a place for Luke. He has furnished it with a single cot, sleeping bag, spool table, battery lamp, bucket, and a jug of water. He uses the basement only in twister weather, when sirens make him run for cover. Then he stores some of his sound equipment downstairs. He has thousands of dollars in equipment. Almost everything he has, though, is in his fingers and body. He doesn't dwell on that much, because he is a modest man, and a superstitious one. If he counts himself too highly, he will be brought low. He likes being known as the best musician around, which he thinks he really might be, yet he doesn't enter contests. Competing makes him far too tense and he isn't going to play worse than he can just to prove he isn't as calm as the next man. He is fine-tuned himself, apt to tremble in the grip of high stress. He has reinforced every wall in the house. It is as sturdy as his talent and hope can make it.

He should have waited on the ladies' arrival yesterday afternoon and made certain they were settled in. Now, with sleet and dropping temperature, they might not be able to drive out even if they wished to. The little bridge would be really hazardous. Just a nervous tic could slide the vehicle and leave it and them hanging over the side. They'd be on foot.

As ice creeps over the land, his kindness and concern for others make him act. He crawls into his blue truck. A coat, gloves in a pocket, lies in the seat beside him. He wears one shirt under his clean overalls and three on top. They can be peeled if he overheats and reassembled in a jiffy. The truck, a real gas-eater, can transport all his essential belongings if he ever needs that, and he can be of assistance to family and friends. And to the community, as now. He keeps the truck running as smoothly as his instruments play.

Having made up his mind, he drives toward Sedalia, enjoying the glow and blend of traffic lights in the frozen air, the silver beauty of trees. Cars are few, like alien travelers. He hums, whistles, feeling competent and strong in this testy situation. There come unbidden to him the lyrics of old songs about love gone awry and women dying, "Sweetwater," "Little Omie Wise," "Knoxville Girl," "Lady by the Sea." Women are vulnerable. Their little strengths and loving ways. He himself will be a warrior for them if they are in danger and if the danger is something he can fight. He doesn't mind a challenge.

The sky is a solid gray sheet. On the highway, two cars are off the edge, the people getting into a trooper's car. At the road to the house, he drives cautiously over the icy span of bridge, shifts into low. He makes it over half-way up. The truck rests at an angle across the road, one rear tire spinning free. He gets out of the truck, walks in a profound, beautiful silence up the grade. The sheer extremity of the moment brings a smile to his face. He's grateful for his sureness of foot and his good wind.

# SATURDAY,
# LATE AFTERNOON

## ANNA

**I'm in the** room I shared with William. The hat tree guards the door to the hall. Connie's luggage lies on the floor, and I kneel by it. I touch the latch, and almost feel it, do feel it, but can't move it. I give myself patience, ease, believing and expecting. The latch springs open. With fingers of both hands lifting upward, I raise the lid! I have succeeded! I push aside a piece of clothing, heavy cotton, black, and see a blue vial, and many clear containers holding pastilles. Most of the containers have paper affixed with a date and name of the medication. The dates are years apart. Connie saves medications? To fight death or find it?

A pale light sweeps upward across the window. What if someone comes for them?

I will be left here, with no help, no sanctuary. Time isn't slow in their world. They could leave me in a moment. That is what I should want—only that. I want to be down with them immediately. Thought has no power at this moment. I try to hurry down the stairs, as I once hurried, fleet of foot—and I do. They might hear me, might catch just a glimpse of who I was, may still be. I want them to know me. They are ill at ease. I may be the cause.

Seated in the needlepoint side-chair, Deborah clutches her coat and purse on her lap, hunches over them. Shelley sits at Deborah's feet. They are nearly of a size, I see, fair haired and dark, one unpolished, the other too polished, similar in some ways. Unmarried and married, both unhappy. Yearning. Is that what he sees in all of them? All of us? Yearning. Are we so hungry? Oh. I would be one of their number, but I have a son, and the hope of William.

Rachel has a camera and gestures toward the music room. "I'm going to get a photo or two of that . . . attic room we found. I'll be back in a jiffy. If I'm not," she addresses Melody directly, "you come after me, okay? Let me borrow your wrist light. Give me thirty minutes. And you, Deborah," she turns toward her, "hang around. We'll get you home tonight if we have to. Nothing has actually happened. We've just read about murders that may have occurred. We could do that anywhere, anytime. Why be more scared here, huh?"

"We're not reading about the ice," Deborah counters. "It's here and now. We're getting imprisoned. Immobilized." She nods toward the box where my son's ostensible belongings are. "And that stuff happened, too. Melody knows it. So does Shelley. Right, Shelley?"

"It could have happened."

"You need to take something, Deb," Connie says. "You're coiled as tight as a spring. You want me to get you something?"

"Not yet. Too much wine makes my face swell. I have a rash on my shoulders, too."

"You should have told me," Connie says. "Red wine does that to a lot of people. I'll bring you a little white wine."

I follow her into the kitchen. My footsteps seem firmer, as if I really walk on these floors, make a small wake in the world. Connie pulls a bottle toward her. It is already partially uncorked. She works the cork out while she watches the doorway. From her pants pocket she takes a handful of small items, a square box, a green vial, a folded paper. She keeps the paper and tucks the other things back into her pocket. The vial catches at the seam. She doesn't notice, unfolds the paper, angles it above an empty glass. Apparently she will calm Deborah against Deborah's will. Just as the powder begins to slide, she tilts the paper up, spilling some on her shirt. She twists the paper on itself, slips it in her pocket. She grasps the sink edge, bows her head, and stands there. She rinses out the glass, dries it. She dampens a napkin and presses it to her face and cheeks. She has stopped herself.

Rachel's voice from the great room distracts me. "I'm going in the passage for a little while. Don't close it."

Then I am somewhere in the passage. I have preceded Rachel, acting on an impulse before I recognized it in myself. Rachel approaches. She has a heavy step. Her goal is obvious. I wish her not to proceed, not to photograph me where I lie dead, not clean, not wholesome. Worn. Lying with guilt. I wish her to think better of her own doings. I block her path, though she could probably walk through me. We are, in physical space, no more than three feet apart. The air must be cool here, with the tiny holes along the eave. I don't speak aloud. We are close. I wonder if she knows my thoughts, knows my nature. Can I alone sway her, at least her?

"Who are you?" she asks, and I am taken aback. Then I am grateful. I bring my hand to my heart. "Anna."

Does she hear? She turns her head as if listening.

"Anna," I say again.

Soon she runs the wrist light up and down where I stand as if she does see me. The air roils.

She says, "I guess I'm not supposed to go on, is that it?"

"Not with the purpose you have."

We are silent together. In a while, she speaks, "I know you're there and don't want me to proceed. You're not him, that's for sure. And thank God for that." She waits again, turns as if to walk away, and fumbles at her waist.

She suddenly faces me and a sharp light flashes between us. She hurries off, a slight run. She has betrayed me by trickery. She has taken my photograph against my will. I hear her labored breathing as she hurries back to her friends. She is frightened of me. I don't wish her to be frightened. She's a creature, too. She has no protection. She desisted as I wanted and turned around. She was brave. Is brave. How does she differ from me? She wants to know with what she deals. My own budding anger dissipates. I could never hold anger long, except at myself.

She has my photograph, yet I don't know what she will see. She may know more of me than I do.

I believe he is elsewhere — outside. He can't be in two places at once, and that is a comfort.

When Rachel joins the women, I am with them. She mutters, "I changed my mind, gals. That place is pretty spooky when you're by yourself." She sits on the floor near the fireplace, faces out to the great room, places the camera next to her. She smiles at Deborah. "See, I get scared, too." She lights a cigarette, exhales the smoke toward the fire. Her gaze drifts across the room. Does she look for me? Where is her mind? Will she help me, us? Or only herself? Have I misread her as one of the good?

Connie slumps on the red davenport. Her legs are stretched out before her, crossed at the ankles, and one short stocking crumpled past the ankle. She has little flesh on her body. Her left pocket is not visible. It needn't be. From my vantage, I can see the kitchen floor just beyond the nearest doorway. In the seam of floor and wall is a splash of green.

The thing has fallen from her pocket. The vial.

I must have it! It has come to my attention and must carry no good and thus I must manage to grasp it up and hold it. Keep it away from all the women, even Connie. And Rachel. I have no doubt that is what I must do. Everything matters when he plays. There are no accidents that are not opportunities. I hurry toward it.

When I stoop to get the vial, a piece of amber thread swirls away. I am captivated. My movement affects the world, even though so tiny a result. I blow at the thread. I think it trembles, but this house is old. Drafts come and go.

In the other room, Shelley suggests again that they begin the stories.

I try to grasp the vial. I can feel it against my fingertips, the delicate curve of it slipping away. It will not be lifted. I have merely nudged it, as if it scoots from me, as if it is a feather and I the breeze. I attempt to lift it, fingertips to each end. No. I did have it. Something stalls me. I hear Shelley's voice. She is beginning her story. I stand erect and am weary from my efforts. How can that be? What in me can be weary? The elusive vial lies in the shallow groove where the threshold begins.

Shelley has dragged a footstool before the fireplace. Once the cover was a miniature group of goldfinches, hovering over a branch of white blossoms. Now the art frays into its substance. The threads separate, flatten, curl. I didn't embroider the piece—my fingers weren't meant for intricate work. They're skinny and the knuckles knotted. The footstool was mine, and it has lasted, even if not quite lovely. For Shelley it is a table on which to place the tools of her story, a camera and a transparent bag of photographs. These are women who seek proof. I did the same. I still do. I long to know. I join them.

SATURDAY,
EARLY EVENING
THE WOMEN

**Shelley's photographs are** passed first to Melody and last to Connie, who, seated in her favored brocade chair, scrutinizes every detail, front and back. There are no notes. Wherever Shelley appears, an oddity does as well, visible in one photo and not another, or in a different location though in the same setting—tiny red bursts, cracks in a wall or vase, a dead flower. Floating spheres of various sizes, much like water bubbles, only much clearer, hold a shifting shadow—something caught or coming into form. In one photo, a stocky woman in a beltless, baggy, print dress and wearing heavy black shoes is to Shelley's left. The woman's features are bland and somewhat blurred, and her dress colorless. Shelley's image is colorful—a red shirt and brown pants and red shoes with straps across her high arched feet. The woman seems a servant or a relative. A grandmother? How can Shelley be in color and the woman not? Are they one community, traveling side by side or merging in a flash of time?

One photo differs. A sole woman commands the same setting. Her yellow blouse dips low, the red skirt flows like silk over knees and down to the floor. Her blonde hair is pulled loosely up and back from a face beautifully symmetrical. The eyes appear dark brown, soft and luminous. A lively, sultry woman. A force.

"Is this woman your mother?" Melody asks Shelley.

"Yes."

"Very beautiful."

"Yes, she was."

"There's nothing strange in this picture," Melody says. Who took this one? Who had the camera?"

"I did. She showed me how."

"Did she ever explain the weird effects in photos of you?"

Shelley sighs. "Yes, in a way. She said some of them are disturbances in the air, the surroundings, like lightning that doesn't strike. I shouldn't worry about them, shouldn't talk about them or to them, or try to dispel them. I should *ignore* them. I don't want to hide or pretend, which is why I'm sharing with you. I don't know what they are, really, or what I am." She turns her face toward Connie. "I want you to know me as I am. I'm a simple person. That's what I choose."

"Your mother's power may have caused what's in the photos of you. Her projection."

"No. She was a good mother. If she could have told me more, she would have. She was honest with me. She could tell fortunes. We owned a grocery store. If a customer hung around till others were gone, my mother would get a shawl, and wait near the back room, which was curtained off. She had a little table and chairs there, a wick lamp, cards, some flat stones. My mother said people want only to hear good things. If I chose to tell futures, I must learn what not to share or how to do it. When a carnival came to town every summer, we would close the store and she would set up a booth with the carnival. They always allowed her to do that. She would bring home a lot of money. More than we could make in the store. 'Make life exciting, not frightening,' she said. 'Warn carefully of dangers. A person shouldn't live in dread.' She wanted me to be happy. She used to prompt me with 'Smile, honey.' I didn't like to smile. It was pretending. She told my fortune, and promised she wouldn't lie to me. She said I would have three brushes with death, but would live a long, long time, and come to happiness."

"How did she tell your fortune?" Connie asks.

"By looking at me." Shelley corrects herself quickly. "She read my palm."

"Can you do it?"

"No. It's a special ability and controlling it may take years of practice."

Connie considers her own palm, rubs it with her thumb. "I'll bet you can. Try it with me."

"I'd rather not."

"Please. Read my palm."

"Don't urge her to do it if she doesn't want to," Melody says. "Maybe she would have to tell you something you don't want to hear."

"I don't care how bad it is. If she can tell me anything, I want to know. Please. Shelley."

Shelley remains by the footstool, arms crossed over her midriff, staring at Connie. "All right," she says. Her features soften as if she might be fading into sleep or daydream, yet her eyes are open and fixed on Connie. She rises and carefully steps by Melody and between Rachel and Deborah, stops before Connie's chair. She takes Connie's hands in her own, holds them without looking at the palms. She closes her eyes and bows her head. The women can't see her face. Connie can. Shelley's cheeks have flushed an ugly red. Her lips quiver. She doesn't speak or move.

"Shelley," Melody whispers "Dear girl. Shelley. Stop, honey."

Shelley turns, startled, to face Melody for a long moment, then back to Connie. She trails a finger over the lines of Connie's palm. With a light caress and smile, she releases the hand.

"Tell me what you see."

"You're fine. You're safe."

"Please, Shelley. Tell me what you know. It isn't fair to almost tell me by action — to hint."

Shelley hugs herself. "Why must I say it? You know you're not well. I can't do anything about it."

"Just answer. Be straight. What's going to happen to me? When?"

"I don't know that. I know the body is failing. It's fading. I know also these good things. The heart and head lines are separate, not fused. You reason well. You're not easily swayed by emotions, and when your mind gives you freedom, you can abandon yourself. The life line is strong and unbroken. No one can promise the length of a life. There are *no* terrible signs. You have a good nature, a good heart. Only the body fails."

The voice is Shelley's. Hesitant, sweet and raspy, spoken in the now. But she's different. There's a distance, like an echo of herself. Something in her has shifted close to an edge.

"Let me try." Rachel grasps Connie's left hand, contemplates the palm somberly. "All right. There's a break near the beginning, just here, under the index finger. You had a close brush with death when you were very young. And . . . " She lowers the hand into the fire's glow. "And here is another break, before the base of the thumb. It's hidden unless the skin is stretched. See? See?" She consults

Connie's face, realizes she's causing pain. "I'm an idiot, aren't I?" She closes the hand as she has seen Shelley do. "Sorry. Whatever it is, I'm sure it's a long way off."

"No need to apologize," Connie says. "I've hoped for an early death most of my life and now I'm old it can't come early, and never early enough."

Silence follows until Deborah's voice, unusually tender, breaks it. "I imagine each of us has at least once thought death might be preferable to where we are."

Melody puts her arms around Shelley and hugs her. She turns back. "We shouldn't have done this. It was too hard on her, especially now."

"I'm all right," Shelley says. "I want to help."

# ANNA

**I understand wanting** to die, even in the young, when, one hopes, it would be only a fleeting thought. Death can appear a wonderland to the wretched. My mother died when I was eight, and I planned to die, too. I fell asleep with a prayer, expecting to wake in that other world, where all was peace and love. Where my mother sang with angels and strolled with the father she hadn't named and I never saw. I woke instead to an eventual short trip to an orphanage where there was no surplus of anything good. It was a stone building. Gray and brown and bare with hazy windows and splintery wood floors and hard cots. I learned to help prepare food, to stoke fires outside for boiling water and washing clothes so coarsely clean they rotted, and to sew, to tie off thread with a twist of it between thumb and finger and to bite it free without getting it moist. One dishtowel was always folded and not used, to indicate our cleanliness. The damp one hung from a nail out of sight.

From where I sit with the women, I see the mudroom

entry and at its threshold the green vial.

"Are you going to tell a story," Deborah asks Shelley, "or was that it? Would you like to stop all this now?"

"No, I don't want to stop. I want to tell my story before we leave. So does Connie, I know."

"Then, I'm going to start the car, let it run for a few minutes to warm up."

I realize Deborah will see the vial. She will take it up. That is what he intends to happen. As I brush by her, she frowns as if my intent did stall her. I'm kneeling and my fumbling fingers have touched the glass. It is rising! I hear Deborah's slight intake of breath. She believes she has accidentally kicked it out of sight. I drop it, not deliberately, and Deborah spies it, bends and picks it up nimbly. She doesn't doubt her senses as I do. She has the thing. She is pleased with it. I want to slap it from her. I think she'll turn, ask the others to whom this belongs. She doesn't. She puts the vial in her coat pocket, collects her purse, and goes through the mudroom and out the door. I have failed twice in the smallest endeavor. I follow to that outer door, listen. Someone is out there, not yet near. I hear, too, the sharp crackling of limbs fragmenting, giving up bark, splitting from the trunk. I hear something else, a man's voice. Not William's.

The others wait for the sound of the car. It doesn't come.

"If the battery's dead, she's going to be livid."

"She may be striking out on foot."

"She's not that foolish."

The door creaks open, and Deborah's pert face appears. She stamps her feet on the mat and advances brightly into the great room. "We all have to be happy campers. We're really stuck here. The car doesn't even groan. No battery at all."

"Did we leave the lights on?"

"No. Well, maybe I did. If so, I don't remember turning them on earlier. The only reason I'm not screaming bloody murder is that when I first went out, I saw just a flash of headlight. I think that's what it was, and I heard scuffing, someone on foot, not far down the road."

"Damn," Rachel says.

Waiting to tell her story, Shelley is downcast. She watches the others peek out the side windows, waiting for whomever might arrive. She wants them not only to listen to her, but to want to listen. I do want to hear. I would invite her. She longs for her companions to care.

"I don't think anyone's coming," Melody says. "Regardless, we need nourishment." She looks fondly at Shelley. "And you, just be patient for a while longer, all right? We'll get to your story. I promise."

"I'm used to waiting."

# SATURDAY EVENING, SUPPER
# THE WOMEN

**The women decide** to take this supper in the main dining room. A mahogany table reaches almost wall to wall, seats ten. Above a matching sideboard hangs a tapestry of many children dancing around a maypole. Fiber damage and poor lighting flatten the rich colors but it's a homey scene to Melody, revealing that the family who hung the tapestry loved children, as she does. It may be repairable in the hands of a talented weaver. Melody has prepared pizza loaves and cut them in small portions, accompanied them with a platter of sliced fresh fruit. Four of the women are aware that pinholes high in this room allow someone in the passage to watch what occurs, and they know, too, of a woman's body in the attic, oddly preserved. They all, even Deborah, have read of death, torture, injury, and have seen sketches by a real person of horrible acts. Though the women are comfortable with each other, and the meal is a normal occurrence, the atmosphere differs among them: Ominous to Deborah. Promising to Rachel and Connie. Pending to Melody and Shelley.

They each know a ghost, at least, is in the house.

"Do you have a cross?" Deborah asks.

"At home," Melody says. "I have a pocketknife with me."

A little laugh comes from Rachel.

"Last supper," Connie says, unable to resist. They do smile and she's encouraged. "I have a cross." She lifts the chain at her neck. "I bought it because we were going to talk about ghosts and while I hoped to see one, and still do, I was wary. I always have safety nets with me. After seeing those sketches—murdered women—I'm very glad to have the cross. I also brought along a vial of holy water. I got it from the entry basin at the old Sacred Heart church. I'll share it if we need it. It can't hurt. Good is good, whatever the source."

"I wouldn't use it," Rachel says. "I'm not a hypocrite. It'd probably burn a hole in me, if, that is, it truly had any power. And what's in the box can't hurt you unless you think too much about it and make yourself ill."

Deborah fondles the vial hidden deep in her skirt pocket. Holy water. She's glad to have it and will give it back to Connie. She likes what Connie said about good.

Their voices are soft and sharing. With Connie's urging, they talk about what might continue after death, about evil spirits, if God made them or if they came from men, if evil was just disease or a life form itself—many life forms. If there was such a being as the comforter—that person people see when they're near death. The person always with you, whether second or third or fourth.

"Never a woman?" Rachel asks.

"Sometimes," Connie responds. "Depends on the belief."

If Shelley acquiesces to what her mind and body can do, she might die. She can feel the power of the house and of each woman, fleetingly, like scents that pass on the tip of a memory. She listens to feelings. There are so many! She longs to respond.

Deborah thinks of Sancho Panza refusing to join Don Quixote's table. A person wants to stay where the rules are clear and the guests known and should thus not *always* seek inclusion. Melody recalls the title of a ballad. Rachel recalls asking for names and stating her own. She isn't sure what she has done or is doing. It doesn't matter, actually. She is what she is and is going forward.

"Six o'clock," she says. "Time for Shelley's story."

"It's pitch-black outside," from Deborah, matter-of-factly.

"Night is night, girl," Rachel replies. "This is daytime no matter what it looks like. And we're almost home."

# SHELLEY'S STORY

**Shelley rearranges her** earlier spot before the fireplace, on the floor, with a square, black-tasseled couch pillow to one side and the footstool on the other. Seated, though, and surveying her friends and the staircase and landing behind and above them, she says, "Let me change this," and quickly plants herself in the center of the fireplace skirt, positioning the two personal boundary markers closer. She can barely contain her story. It threatens to burst out in gibberish. She must take one thread and uncoil it slowly so the other threads can be seen. Control is a secret one learns and practices as she has. Sectioned moments and movement. Increments that do not shift others. "Thank you for waiting. I hope I don't block the heat." She resists the impulse to look behind her, into the fire, and through it, into the dining room. She slows her breathing.

"My story happened inside a house," she begins, "not like yours."

The women are surprised.

"She's right," Connie says. "Rachel was driving at night and stopped near the site of a murder. Deborah was at the ruins of a house where a woman had been murdered. Melody was at a cemetery and neared the grave of a woman who had burned to death, maybe murdered. All outside."

"What about you, Connie?" Rachel asks.

"I'd rather save that till I tell my story. We have an interesting order developing. You go ahead, Shelley."

"Mine was that Victorian house just east of our post office in Mason. People have painted it many colors over the years, now lavender and green, a very unusual combination, but attractive. It has the traits that sell an old house—gabled dormers and gingerbread trim, a white porch in front and around one side, and always in good repair. Cared for. I saw the house often because in nice weather when I go after the company's post-office-box mail, I walk. On two days this past summer, I saw a man at the upper window, washing or scraping the glass. I assumed he was a handyman, and the house was going on the market. The third day, he wasn't in view, and I wanted to see inside. I tried the front door, then went round to the back. Chrysanthemums bordered the brick walkway. Honeysuckle and wisteria covered the small yard. The perfume was so heavy I became dizzy and sat down on the edge of the porch. It slanted toward the yard, which I knew was to keep rain or melted snow from running toward the house, but I felt that it slanted also to keep me away, toss me to the yard. I didn't want to miss my opportunity to see the interior. When the dizziness eased, I tried the door. Unlocked.

"Never have I seen a house so clean. Bright and stark, newly painted—a muted yellow downstairs. A loud voice seemed wrong, so I didn't announce my presence. My shoes probably made sound. I was tremendously curious. I moved through the rooms of the ground level slowly, confident the man I had seen would be upstairs. The floors below were narrow dark oak, the grain like running black needles. No scrapes. No damage in any room. No furniture. There were two staircases, a main one on the east side, wide, with deep steps, and another near the kitchen, steep and shallow steps—servant stairs. Sometimes, the servants' staircase is behind the wall with a small door into the kitchen. Not a secret passage, just hidden to separate the workings of a house from its social life. I knew there might be a third staircase, too, from outside, or from the basement. I know houses."

Shelley has been able to see her friends' faces, the seating in general, and the swaying and weaving of shadows from lamps and the firebox. Now the breakfront draws her gaze because its center blurs while the two glass panels on either side are clear. Something stands there. Without moving her body or her eyes she allows her vision to see all of the room before her. Only one more ghost, kneeling or sitting by Shelley's photos and the empty packet that held them.

"Since the wide staircase had no runners, I must have made noise. I thought he might come to the landing. I went into the bedroom directly ahead, which held the window I had seen him in. He had to be tall, considering the angle of my view. There was no ladder, no stool, no tools at all. No dust. No sign of human life. I passed the next room without entering. A house has its own strengths. Some crumble. Others turn stone-like, stubborn and solid. Rooms, too. Fight. Seal off. Cringe. The next room was very small. To my left was a pale blue wall with a tiny door just off-center. It was black, with a glass doorknob—clear glass, not white like the others. The black didn't match the room at all. I thought the door might give to a dormer or a wood bin. All the old houses had coal or wood bins, upstairs and down. I wasn't dreaming. I could hear street traffic and could see branches of a walnut tree outside. It was the same sunny day I had come from. A real day. Time was passing as it does pass, not dream time.

"I turned the clear knob, inched the door to me. I saw this person my own size, with wild hair and black pants and a red shirt, white skinny arms. It was me. Before me was a white-framed, full-length mirror exactly my height. The reflection was mine. Then another reflection stepped into it, behind me. Someone tall and dressed in brown. He clamped his skinny fingers on my shoulder. I jerked down and away. He had a bloody knife. What I thought was a knife. I scrambled by him, to the hallway, down the stairs and saw him there, at the bottom of the other stairs. He couldn't have been there first. Impossible. I ran toward the kitchen, the way I had come in, realized he was closest, and, as soon as he ran that way, I darted back to the front and got to the entrance, unbolted it, and out. I had outfoxed him.

"I remember his appearance perfectly. He was very young, a teenager. Thin. His eyes were hard, though. Very cold. Pellet eyes. He had locked on me. He had just killed someone, that's what I thought. He had just killed some woman and she was hidden somewhere in the house. What if she wasn't dead, and I was standing around doing nothing? There was a stillness about the place. I remembered that the knife was bloody, so why was there no blood in the room? He could have as easily come after me as have gone the other way. I wondered why he hadn't. Maybe he wasn't worried because he hadn't actually done anything and I only thought the knife was bloody. Maybe it wasn't a knife at all but a paintbrush.

"I crept around the house's perimeter. I peeked into the basement. Everything was visible. The house was like a huge yellow cage, with something flitting around, always perching where I wasn't looking. Not hidden ever, just not there at that moment." Shelley stops. She blinks, shakes her head. "That's enough," she says. "That's all I have."

"What did you do? You at least called the police, right?"

"Yes, I did. I'd left my phone at the office. I called the police from the post office. The manager let me use the phone. I went back and waited across the street. Even if he left before they arrived, he couldn't have cleaned up . . . whatever. If there had been any."

"Unless the blood was from another place, and he was hiding there."

"The officers didn't find anything. They went through the house I don't know how many times. They scoured neighborhood yards, too. That's what was on the radio and the television. They had scoured the neighborhood."

"What do you think it was, Shelley?" from Connie. "A vision? A psychic experience?" She bites her lip, then adds, "An episode?"

"I don't know what kind of experience it's called," Shelley replies. "It was real. I think he had killed someone and wanted to kill me."

"He could have, couldn't he, if he was real? He was close enough. You said yourself he could move faster than you."

"He made a mistake. I'm fast enough and sly when I must be. I got away."

Deborah, gaze fixed on Shelley, blinks, turns to Melody. "Don't you tell us someone was killed in that house, too."

"All right," Melody returns. "I won't tell you."

"When?" Rachel.

"I don't remember the year. I know he had been a guest at a dinner party. He left with another guest but managed to get back in and up to the child's bedroom. He carried her to the basement."

"That's the worst one yet," Deborah cries.

"Yes," Shelley says. "It is. I have another picture for you." Shelley takes up her camera, opens the viewing screen. "I took this last night." She gives the camera to Melody.

Melody stares puzzled at the tiny window. "I'm not sure I see it. You photographed a mirror, right? That shape could just be a trick of the mirror. Old mirrors have mercury in them and as they age, the distribution of the mercury changes. This could be a change in the mirror itself. Not a reflection. But we shouldn't discount it. Shelley knows what she's talking about."

Rachel takes the device, looking at the image while she adjusts the setting. "I can make out a shape. It's vague, but something *is* hanging there. Even if it's caused by mercury, we'll save it. It has features. It'll print out."

"Do you see where I might fit in?" Shelley asks,

assertively for her, and sad. "I go through all the rooms in the house. I peek through all the windows. I've shared photos with you. And I have this photo. It *is* a ghost." She looks toward the breakfront and one of the blurs slips to the side. The other remains where it was. "I don't know everything. I can't. But there are at least two beings in this house besides us, and I took a picture of one. A bad one."

"Oh." Rachel's eyes poll the others. "Okay. We believe you. We'll be leaving soon, hon. We're almost gone. Besides, we don't have to *fear* them, Shelley. Knowing about them doesn't mean running from them. Ignore them, like your mother said."

# *SATURDAY, MIDEVENING*

## *JOHN*

**The musician Luke** has left his vehicle, his truck, which is his armor against the ice and the cold. He picks his way cautiously on his stick legs. The moon our light bathes us equally. His breath is white, little steams of will.

What he thinks to do with five of them loose clinging to his savior's arm I do not know. He frightens them, he saves them. So goes humanity.

If I could spend myself into nothing, as he can, I would not do it, I think I would not do it. How can I know until the opportunity presents itself? I can't plan it or arrange it. Can't create it. I can use it. I can abide in a thought and act just as I can abide in an object or body.

He slips here. He slips there. He catches himself

*with fingertips, a dance of bravery. He goes upward again. The house that holds them is alight. So it used to be nightly. Ice encircles the wires to the house, ice weights the limbs around the wires. The night prepares, acts as it will.*

*Luke, fellow. Tread on.*

*He does not know how far he can reach. In that, we are the same. I don't know who made me.*

*Let us say I made myself. I make the claim.*

*I want Anna to stay. She is parcel to the site. She is a tree rooted here, the waterway beneath, the moon above, the plants that come and go in seasons. She is where I return when I must, when my travels cease. What carves out my path? How do I traverse beyond where I am, to where I will? My little passages worry a crevice here, erode a channel there, and Lo! Lo! I have furthered myself. Perhaps. That is my theory. An eternity in inches. Perhaps I aspire to my creator.*

*Anna saw me. She chose me. She spied and probed and surprised. Aha! Woman. You have me. You have me. Anna.*

*She wonders what happened to her William, that mound of man. He set forth one day, with a one-*

*equine wagon, set forth to bring home a brown sewing machine from Goodie store. And is no more.*

*Perhaps the big man drove the mare west. Along the road to Mason — a line for a tune — along the road to Mason walked a pretty girl. She waved him to stop and that he did. There was a touch of too much flesh to the lady, too much this and that. She watched him from the corners of her doe-like eyes. She was running away, she was. Fleeing the ugliest street in the town behind them where she had earned her livelihood with all she had. She adored him with her eyes, hungry, scared little being. Angry little creature. He was a big man, a protector, not lusting for her, shying away. A smart fellow. Judging her too harshly, wasn't he? Pout. Pout. She wooed him to draw the wagon off road, down toward a copse near the channel, so she could seek some privacy. He acquiesced. What could he do? At the copse, she didn't leave the wagon immediately. With the snow melting, and the soil softening, and the little stones separating to trap narrow shoes and wheels, she laid her hand upon his thigh. Laid her hand. Spoke "You're a handsome gentleman" and stirred her fingers to stir him.*

*"We'll have none of that," he said. He was a man, all hair and horn as they are, and alas, he did not turn astray. He told her, "Get down, out of the wagon. Ride with someone else." She obeyed, slapping soundly the flank of the horse which bolted only enough to tilt the wagon and drag it with him holding the reins, out of his senses, coldcocked, not dead, mashed in the face as the wagon flipped. Mouth agape, the miss feared her handy work. She prodded the man. William the man. She emptied his pockets. The horse shuddered and shied. She dragged the man by both feet, then one, then the other, resting, dragging, resting, till she brought him to the edge of the creek. Ice floated on the surface, thinning. She turned the body so she could push it like a plow onto the ice and its weight cracked an opening and the torso sank, sank. When she had, with a makeshift pole, prodded it down and out of sight, she turned to the horse. She cooed it quiet. She unfastened it, led it back to the road. Near the copse below was a jumble of dark that could have been a wagon if one were searching for it. She mounted the animal, wary at so much power between her legs, and continued fleeing slowly, toward the next little town and a larger*

*one beyond. The man, William, had worn heavy shoes. One of them lodged beneath a root. His calf was caught. His entire body was sheltered in a network of roots, inanimate cage. No one found the wagon. The winter came on again, then spring, with high water and powerful winds. Boards were scattered, floated. Bones appeared, traveled inches away one day and the next.*

*Or . . .*

*Perhaps he drove east and visited there a particular street and a particular female. They could not have enough of each other and so they left together, left mewling Anna and the crazed boy behind, to query and struggle. The same female that could have hailed the wagon.*

*Or . . .*

*Perhaps a remnant of war was passing through and he disliked the very sight of a complacent resident like William with a good horse and wagon and probably money in his pocket, disliked it so much that he shot the center of the image from behind, the bullet to the center of the cranium. He scalped our William, took the fat wallet, wrapped the body in a blanket intended to shield something else, drove the wagon to the*

*Blackwater and there let the body sail down to the sluggish water where it snagged eventually in the roots of a cypress.*

*Or . . .*

*Perhaps the boy son, the love-cripple, waited at the first turn from the house, and rode along with his father. In that eventuality the wagon and horse were sold and only the boy knows how the father met his end. I may know where the corpse decayed and fed fowl or fishies.*

*The musician. Luke. Admirable male. Comely as humans see themselves. Striving up the hill, up the hill, where the dainties await.*

*I enjoy this place. I soar.*

# ANNA

**I am in** my shattered room. The crosses still hang in the windows, on the propped door. It is night, the world is more silver than black. Ice reflects the bright moon. We could all be encased under ice, under glass. I long to be in a final place and know myself. He listens and listens. Is he learning more than I am? I know he learns and adapts. As do we all, and should.

When William and I came here, we searched the house over, deciding to purchase it even though he was establishing a store in town. We went to the cellar together. It seemed sound enough to him—stone walls and a dirt floor. Shelves near the stairs held a few jars, all filled. "Don't be feeding that stuff to me," William joked.

The body knows evil, if not the source. The jars held poison. There were no labels, but near the neck of the jar had been scratched an x. The jars were dirty and that dirt was a warning. They had been unearthed and placed there. Something precious.

During any time a reason for killing can arise—pests,

wild and dangerous creatures. Enemies. The war was only two years over then. Someone living here during the war, or even before, had planned protection, and maybe used it. Destroying the jars' contents was dangerous, and may have been the reason for keeping them. Some poisons are airborne. They can be inhaled or absorbed through the skin, fall into water. People die every day in some part of the world. Poisons don't have to kill to destroy.

"They're spices," I told William. "I'll see to them. They must be moldy."

I hid them. Better to have them in case they were needed.

I had learned about poisons as I had learned about God and sacrifice, and sparrows, and valleys of death, and the temple of the body, and think on all things virtuous and good. Even the beneficial can bring mild harm—and worse in ignorant or skilled hands. Jonquil, Morning Glory, Chestnut, Apple, Peach. Berries. The humble potato. Some poisons are nearby and meant for the worst harm. Oleander. Belladonna. Water hemlock. Wolfsbane. Castor Bean. What doesn't grow in one's own land can be bought or bartered for, combined, stored, dried, powdered. As medicine is available every season, world over, so is poison—often from the same substance. God planned it so. We have to use our judgment.

The day William didn't return was just before spring,

in a thaw. Our son's body had healed, the canes shut away.

"Come with me," William had said to John.

John declined. "It's a good day to be out drawing. "

"Draw what's along the road. Do something in town. There's lots to see every place and every minute. It doesn't have to be on this property."

"I like it here better," John said.

I believed John stayed on our land. I saw him in the field at least twice that day, heard him upstairs, though I didn't hear him come into the house.

"Come have some soup," I called up the stairs. There was no answer and I went up, quietly. I had fallen into spying. Outside his door, I said "John?" and he answered. "Yes Ma'am," which I hated. To call his mother Ma'am.

I told him there was food waiting, soup and some cold roast I could warm up if he wanted.

"No, thank you. I'm going back out in a while."

"Come spend some time with me."

He didn't answer and that nettled me. I grasped the doorknob to face him down and tell him he was to come out of his room and have lunch. I became wary of opening the door. I let go the knob and went downstairs. I sewed in the great room, at the small table, and waited for him to come down the stairs. He did not descend. The only time I was not on guard was when I used the privy. He could have gone out then. And he could have gone out through the passage, down into the cellar. He could have done almost anything.

When I went into his room, it was long dark outside, but I wasn't yet alarmed about William. He might not arrive until ten. It was fairly mild, and he might have stayed for supper in Sedalia or worked in the store. In the dusky room, John was asleep on his bed, on his side, facing the door. I could see the clean, unmarred lines of his features. Beautiful young man. His sketchbook was beside him, open, face down. I picked it up. He had drawn a thorn branch with ice encircling the thorns. A small bird perches at the base of the branch — a female cardinal, dark and taut with a crest. Part of the knotty trunk runs down the left side of the page, and toward the bottom a half arc appears, bearing John's initials. In the background is a ribbon of white, like a frozen creek, broken by a jagged hole at its edge and narrowing into the center. From the other bank bare tree limbs draped down as if reaching for something.

John had wakened, was watching me from half-lidded eyes.

"Truly nice," I said, and replaced the book as I had found it. "Your father has not come home. I'm worried."

"He could be all right," he said, as he sat up. He was a lanky boy, too big for that low bed, too much grown to be in a child's room. He seemed strange to me then, and angry.

I wondered suddenly why he had said, "He could be all right," instead of "He is all right." There was a distinction, surely. A difference. He was hinting to me, taunting me with a question. This was the other. Cold eyes.

"Yes." I told him. "He'll be home soon."

I went out and closed the door behind me.

My son hated me. Why wouldn't he? I had tried to kill what was in him, and knew, though I choked to acknowledge it, that I might have tried even if it had meant killing him, too. Why, then, had the other remained? Why would a creature stay with that which had tried to kill it? Did he want me to succeed? Did he know I would ever fail?

William didn't come home.

Now I sit in my sanctuary and, doing as I was once encouraged to do, I take my pen in this weak hand, and I dip it in the ink that is from a time I can't remember. Not the time. Not when. Did John teach me in a moment of freedom? I hold the tip near the paper and recall my past script, which was tiny and crisp. No flourish. I think on one of the faces below and put the pen to paper. I hear the tentative yet lovely scratching and dip the nib again, keep only one face in my mind lest too many stop me. Constance.

Please bury my son in holy ground. Perform rites to save his soul.

Done! Legible to my eyes. To theirs, I can only pray. Will John fly to the heavens, will he be released to oblivion?

What will happen to me? Will I be dragged down and scream forever through the vents and valleys of hell? Are there such torments? Throughout all time? What god would do that? I will choose it to save my boy.

That other is at the door, just beyond sight. He watches me, devours me. He is hungry to know my every move, every thought. Starved to own me. And then? He'll wander, unabated, wanting the unattainable. He is unleashed appetite, ravenous, always seeking. Lapping up souls.

I near the door, peer through the gap between it and frame. Two small points blur and I fix on them. They rise, move toward me. Eyes? I don't know what he is, how he's formed, if he ever truly is. He stands near, huge. I feel a terrible warmth against me, who should have no feeling, feel a touch to my lips and a cupping of my breasts, as if he were William. Never has this happened before. What is in store for me now?

"You'll not have me," I whisper, and reach for the cross that hangs on the door. "Not one of us."

# *JOHN*

**Anna flees from** my stories, but I am close upon her. I am faster than thought and thus faster than she. She finds herself outside the house we share. This she has not intended. I see and sense her shrivel from the vastness of freedom. Yes, it is huge, unending. Sounds reverberate past the stars, even your heartbeat, sweet. One supposes. Around us, close and closer, the frozen world splits and black veins race like snakes. She ventures a few steps farther. To leave, perhaps? To seek someone? She cringes, anxious and fearful. Bright eyed animal. Curious creature. What is this and what must she do? Oh, what will our Anna do? Save somebody, Sughy. Save somebody. Save me.

If I had made myself, I would have a home. It would be a body I could touch. I would be constant, ever the same — this visage here and there and everywhere. I become that which allows *me access. I meet its needs, use its resources. I do not worry about my nature. That is for humans.*

*The musician has taken a tumble, has stumbled off the road into rocks that I didn't make. One arm is lodged crooked between stone, and from his cracked fine skull warm blood seeps onto the ice. I miss him already. I do not wish him to die. I do not wish anything to cease being. I do not wish. Period. Infinity. I long. For ever.*

*Inside, Anna's guests have stoked their fire against the encircling cold night and against me.*

*There was her boy, who told her.*

*"He's left you because of me. I should leave you, too."*

*"Why do you think he left me because of you?"*

*"He told me so, the day he left. He asked me to come with him."*

*She didn't want to believe that, and thus didn't. She stared at her son or at me, twixt the two there's nary a hair, and said, "That day, you said you were sketching in the fields. You said you hadn't seen him."*

*"I lied," he said. And then he cried, very quietly, not a sound at all, only that seeping of tears, a*

signal that always touched her.

"Don't be afraid," she said. "I'll find a way to help you. I'll stay with you until I do."

And so she has.

John could weep. Then he suffered me and now weeps no more.

If Anna knew the musician lay feeding the earth, would she run to his side? No. There was a dog once that yapped and yapped and yapped and snarled at what he couldn't see. I teased him a weaving way, this and that, and he was caught in his own fervor. His chain looped on a jagged root. I didn't chain him or chop the tree that made the root. His yipping became sharper, like pricks into a tender heart. Fainter and fainter and the night grew colder. Anna heard. Dead yet living though she was, human and past human, she heard. Did the sound tear at her? Oh yes indeed. It did. Did she quicken and fly to the dumb animal's aid, seek help, warm its dying flesh? No. Anna cringed inside this very house and guarded her pittance of senses for the sake of her wasted, desiccated, lifeless son. Who lies there in his secret room, all bone and skin and eyes forever closed. Unless I open my own. Fear *is the ice that imprisons her now. Fear of too much power, of horizons unexplored, turns her away, and she fades to join the womankind inside.*

*I am there first and she espies me. She takes a place among the females. The fairest of them all, pale lily, pale death and sacrifice. Baleful glance at me. Be damned either she or I would say.*

# SATURDAY,
# MIDEVENING

# CONNIE'S STORY

**Connie is chilled** to the marrow despite wearing three layers, the top a black crewneck sweater. She angles the brocade chair at one side of the fireplace, settles in and pulls her braid over her shoulder. "I don't want it dangling near a fire," she says, smiling. She's glad to be last and glad they're wrapping up the stories. She believes she sees how the stories come together. She wants to allow the others to understand slowly, to discuss what it could mean. What, if anything, they can do. Should do.

"My ghost story occurs also in Mason, also about two years ago, October. I had made an appointment with a woman who worked in a factory in Industrial Park. She had a reputation as an herb woman, and could provide some treatments that weren't available elsewhere, like bee-sting therapy. She didn't have a car and rode to work with some other women. I was going to pick her up at the factory and take her home later. An accident backed up traffic and I was late—not much, fifteen minutes or so. I was concerned about it. I'm never late. The building was easy to spot—metal, with few windows and a corrugated aluminum roof. Sort of a cheap, functional building. Probably dangerous to work in and owned by a company that didn't pay much. Only a couple cars were there. No one outside. I found the main door locked. I got in my car and honked the horn a couple times. I tried the main door again, knocked, yelled, 'Hello,' and waited a few minutes. You know how it is, not wanting to give up on a meeting you need to occur. You hope circumstance will favor you if you persist. It didn't.

"I drove north, toward the access road by Highway 50, and saw a woman waiting outside the next factory up. I thought I had misunderstood directions, and that was the meeting place. As I parked, the figure disappeared. I assumed she had gone inside, so I followed, announcing my presence by calling her name. The room was huge, crisscrossed with maybe fifty long, wooden tables, each with sewing machines, cloth fragments, large spools of thread. Lint floated as if work had just ended. I could feel it on my cheeks and hands. Fans and ducts overhead indicated the air would be somewhat stirred and maybe filtered throughout the day, but nonetheless—what a slave station. Inoperable, I decided, and illegal—a relic from old factory times. 'Hello,' I called, standing by the second table — unwilling to intrude further. A man appeared at a doorway on the inner left, startling me by the sight alone, but also because I almost knew him. He resembled a fellow who had once frequented the library, tall and ropy, roughly handsome, with a sensuous mouth and hungry eyes. He had a strong scent, not from uncleanliness so much as from excessive maleness.

"I explained why I had come and that I had seen the woman enter the building. He said he would try to catch her for me, and added, pointing to a particular chair, 'You could wait right there.'

"My body warned me. The thought of moving inward had made the ceiling lower, darker, the room tighter, the air too close. I said, 'I have to get home,' but the words sounded muffled. I groped for the door, pulled myself outside. And there he was, waiting for me on the curb. I would have to pass him.

"All my strength went into getting to my car and inside it. You know those dreams in which you can't find the right street, or the shoes you lost, or reach something you need desperately but can't identify? That's what I experienced. To get away, I persisted with one thought in one direction, which is something I can do."

Connie pauses, coughs into her palm, and with a discreet movement of finger and thumb wipes the corners of her mouth. "Only later, brooding about the encounter as I undressed for bed, I realized I might have intercepted a haunting. I had worn a blue blouse."

"How could your blouse matter?" Deborah.

"Because the other woman had worn a blue blouse. She was on her path, returning to the building, but with my arrival she disappeared. I'm the one who entered and who lingered. I took her place."

"Interesting," Rachel says. "Why didn't the guy disappear when the woman did?"

"I thought about that. Maybe he knew—knows—how to remain, or how to recreate the haunting. Maybe a murderer can always revisit his crime, especially if he's a certain type of being. Maybe he uses the haunting as a lure."

"Why would he show you? Particularly you?" Rachel.

"I made myself an audience, and maybe a participant. I came to him."

"Were you really frightened?" Deborah asks.

"Yes. I feared the nearness of him and what he was, of being locked in with ugliness and loneliness, no choice or escape. No way to redeem myself, even to die. Finding another me, and another, and another, and none of them who or what I would be if I could. He was revealing his secret. I've never been able to see anything before. Nor since. I don't have any abilities, not even common ones, and none like Shelley or the rest of you."

"I don't understand," Deborah says. "What does it matter that you came to him? Isn't that the way it always happens? I've never *seen* ghosts either, until that one."

"You also saw him again the same day. You stopped on property where he was, sought a special site from the past. He revealed himself to you, his clothing, his appearance, even his methods. You ran away, approaching another house on the same property. You ran away again, delayed actually leaving, just to look once more. You said so. The next day you phoned and queried. You *pursued*, Deborah."

"I went to a ghost, too," Shelley said. "To the lavender house. Up the stairs."

"Exactly."

"And so did I," Melody says. "At the cemetery. I left the group to seek him out."

"I see what you mean," Deborah says "We all went seeking and we found something. A ghost. Who revealed himself to us."

"Yes."

"Whatever happens to us, we've asked for it?"

"I won't go that far. I'm trying to find a common denominator, because we differ in many ways. We did pursue ghosts, on the day we encountered one, and by coming here."

"I didn't pursue a ghost—if the man I saw *was* a ghost," Rachel says.

"You did cross his path, possibly twice. May I ask what you were coming from?"

"No."

Deborah reenters the conversation. "How do you know, Connie, the man you saw at the factory was a killer? He could have been a prankster ghost. Harmless. He could have just been a man hiding to surprise someone."

"After I saw him, I researched crime reports for that area going back until I found one that fit. Her name was Belle Davis. She was killed in 1956. She had worked overtime and was found a few days later near Knob Noster. She had been killed outside the car, then put back behind the wheel. The police thought the murderer had been waiting for her in the car."

"So why is that important other than it's one more hideous thing?"

"Each of us has seen someone associated with a killing. Probably a murderer. Worse, really."

Deborah lowers herself to the arm of the davenport. "We haven't been describing separate ghosts, have we? We've been describing the same one? The five men are one?"

"It could be. If the timeline is real, and I'm not saying it is, then we could be on the timeline."

"I don't like that a bit. Not a bit." Deborah shakes her head rapidly, blows from pursed lips, waylaying panic.

"Would you rather it was many? At random?"

"In the long run," Melody says, "it doesn't matter. One that can be anywhere anytime or many spreading out. What matters is what part we play. Don't let them do what they plan if you can stop it. Seeing after the fact doesn't help."

"It warns you," Shelley says. "Teaches you."

"Should, at least." Melody shifts attention to Connie. "What about the woman you had planned to meet that afternoon? Was she all right?"

"I called her later. Her ride and friends had waited with her and when I didn't show, the women left together."

"So, the first factory was the right one?"

"Yes. Only the stalled traffic made me late. Chance." She shrugs. "Many variables but one constant—seeking. Openly seeking. Blindly."

# ANNA

**I have wondered** if I am the crazed one and fabricated that other being. And I have wondered if I am he. If I have projected my sickness into an expression I can see and distance myself from and have attached it to my son to rid myself of my own evils. Is evil in the eye of the beholder? Any turn of words can sound true, especially if the turn is smooth enough, and balanced.

I did love the stories the old mistress saved and told, about beings with animal heads and cloven hooves and wild, whipping tails. She was the mother to all of us in the orphanage — not the owner or manager, though they were kind enough. She was cook, and storyteller, and bits of daily gentleness in voice and touch. I loved writing for her when her hands failed, and reading her secret book, her remedies and recipes, how to name an ailment and to cure it, to rout evil or to rouse it. I loved the simple images, the words of plants and herbs and minerals. I loved walking in the common world believing we were surrounded by angels that would descend from the clouds, demons that would rise from the ground, a world filled with the embodiments of spirits—birds who trilled old love songs and stories, maidens transformed to trees, flowers that could blind or bring sight, powders for babes or no babies. Power in fingertips and spoken words. I did not practice. I only copied and listened. "Think on good," my mother had said. "Think on the best you can be and strive to that."

I failed. Fail still. Struggle still, too.

I read of two sisters, Katy and Maggie Fox, who claimed contact with the dead, and who later confessed to lying, and then confessed to the confession having been lie. I read and questioned and considered. And prodded William to guide me. "Would you talk with a spirit if you could?" I insisted. "If you knew for certain it was a real spirit, would you try?"

"If the spirit was yours, Anna, I would try again and again."

He was a good man. I will have it no other way. I have faith in that love. We must sometimes choose a faith. It may be the only comfort.

Sometimes husbands don't come home. The boy never grieves which tortures the mother, wrenches her till she is sick with grief at the mystery of her loss and of her son's coldness—coldness except for that peek of sadness and longing of someone caught in there, fragmentary, rare. Like an infant's silent plea for help.

Sometimes I heard what might have been the creature's voice, a guttural, raspy clucking. He and John would talk. I would approach quietly and see only my son, with his eyes already fixed on where I would appear, and that strange gleam of something peering from deeper in, not John, in John, behind the eyes.

No matter what rumors ran through the community, William would not have abandoned me willingly. He had not visited the women's street in town. He had not killed the girls and blamed their deaths on our boy. And he did not leave me because he feared for his own wellbeing. William did not fear me. Neither did John. Nothing I did made the latter fear me, though it should have.

The sketch I had seen in John's room kept appearing before me. A puzzle. I returned to his room when he was gone. I supposed then he was gone. I can't know. Sketchbooks were on a wooden chair at the foot of his bed, the one I sought on top. I stepped into the hall where the light was brighter and found the puzzling sketch. The arc against the tree—a wagon wheel, broken and fallen away from the wagon. The break in the thin ice beyond wasn't large enough for a wagon to have fallen through—a horse, yes, or a man. Both. The female cardinal. Alone. I understood. With the sketch, John had brought home the story of what happened to his father. He kept it knowing I would find it. I would eventually understand and feel that utter loss again. He had killed his father. He had caused the crash.

Desperate to be wrong, I prayed. Let me be wrong, please? Spare me one or both of the people I love. If not both, then just one. William. If not William, if it's too late, then John. Save him.

I looked at the sketch again. I had missed something. His initials. I touched them and hoped they were blurred, smudged. No. My son's initials were JAB. The artist of this piece was JCB. Through my son but not my son.

**Has it gotten** colder in here?" Melody chafes her upper arms. "I haven't heard the radiators in the last little while. I think they've turned off." She goes to the nearest unit. "It's cooling," she tells them. She crosses the room "This one too. The boiler's off." She smiles wanly and with her right hand at her breast mimes a fluttering heart beneath. "Tell you what, girls, I'll get us more wood, and check out the boiler while I'm at it."

"Not alone," Rachel says. "We all go, or none."

A low stack of dry logs and mottled leaves lines the south wall, near the short steps that ascend to the yard-side cellar door. Melody examines the sides and back of a huge metal machine, opens a rectangular hatch and clangs it shut. "This boiler runs on gas. I bet it's out. There's probably a propane tank somewhere, and it's empty. So be it."

In the far section where Melody now stands, the dirt has been covered with a crude flooring of wide planks, apparently nailed to a square frame. On that surface lies a thin, ragged mattress and jumbled coverings.

"This is where Luke slept." She shines the wrist light at the space above the bed. "Sounds could carry up through gaps in the floor. That music you heard, Connie—he was playing for our benefit all right. In fact," she traces something else in the ceiling, "there's a pull-down frame here—a ladder. This place is riddled like a warren."

She turns the beam onto the flooring.

"What's that?" Rachel has noticed the pipe. "Is the house above a spring?"

"Let's get some extra wood." There's an urgent softness to Melody's voice, as if she must shoo children before her. "The smell down here is foul." She gestures come along to Shelley.

# PART III

# OUTDOORS
# THE WOMEN

**Upstairs, they try** their phones again from both front and rear doors. No service. Rachel risks a few steps onto the ice and gives her phone a shake. "We should at least have emergency service. Ice couldn't shut everything down."

With the outside world crackling and moaning, Deborah, Connie, and Rachel move the davenport, settee, and chairs closer to the fire and to each other, like a closed camp, not so much for safety as to keep heat in, though of course it rises to the high ceiling. Shelley and Melody place the iron fireback to reflect heat only into the great room.

Rachel opens the front door and goes out onto the deep porch. An ice world as far as she can see, silver and black, pristine, beautiful. She hears something. A moan, gentle, like a tremble in the throat. She hears it again and turns quickly to the door. "Someone's hurt out here," she calls.

The others come behind her, eyes searching different directions. The moon is high above the bare sycamore not far from the porch. A limb cracks off as they watch, falls out of sight.

Melody eases her way down the steps, a few inches of her skirt hiked up to free her movements. "I hear it," she says, and carefully picks her way over to the depression where the limb had fallen.

Rachel is off the porch, skittering on ice a second, catching herself. "I'm right behind you."

They're at the edge together, and down almost simultaneously. "It's Luke Essex." Melody starts down. "We may be too late."

"We shouldn't move him," from Rachel.

"We can't call for help and we can't leave him out here. We're bringing him up."

"Get some blankets ready," Rachel calls toward the porch.

Melody stands by the fallen branch. "Get the other end, Rachel. We'll lift and pitch it to the right, my right, your left." She bends her knees and leans forward, grasping the branch just inches from Luke's throat. She takes a deep breath. "Ready." Another breath. "Set." Another. "Go!" They lift and toss the branch aside in one smooth motion, but Melody staggers backward.

"Throw us a blanket," Rachel calls and swiftly Shelley

appears with a quilt, comes to the upper edge near them, and drops it down. It sails, yellow and blue, and crumples on the frozen ground.

Melody breathes raggedly, wheezes, "Let's get him inside."

The two maneuver the body onto the quilt. In the fore, Melody kicks and stomps small snags and she and Rachel together ease up the slope, trying to slide the body gently or lift it over roughness. They dig their shoes in, pull, grunt. Finally at the porch, they are assisted by Connie and Shelley. They lift him to the flat surface, rest briefly. Deborah keeps the door open as they carry him over the threshold and lay him before the single fireplace. Shards of ice mark their path.

His arms, one unnaturally angled, slip from the quilt. Blood mats his black hair in the back and on the right temple. A gash runs over his forehead across the eyebrow, eye, and down onto cheek.

"He was coming to help," Deborah says, her voice quivering. "Poor young man."

Melody presses fingertips to the side of his neck, shakes her head, tries again with her head bowed. She scoots, takes his wrist and feels for the pulse there. "He's very cold. I think we're too late."

"He moaned just minutes ago," Connie reminds her. "That's what got us out here. He may just be in shock. The body reins in and slows down to protect the vital organs. People who have fallen in frozen lakes survive, even when they've been under for a long time. They don't breathe. They hibernate. They preserve the self."

"Then we need to get him some help," Deborah says. "Even if we have to walk. That's the only thing we can do. It's not terribly cold. Things freeze at thirty-three and sometimes I wear just a blazer in that temperature. We can get to town. I know I can. Not alone. With one of you."

In case they're wrong, Rachel kneels by Luke, tilts his head back, and, pinching his nose closed, places her mouth over his and breathes into him, twice, rests, then repeats. Does it again and again. He is sickeningly cold. She shivers. She knows he's dead. She can tell. She breathes into him one more time, sits back on her heels.

"Thanks," Connie says, looking down at Luke's pale face.

Rachel gets up, opens the front door, and stands there, inhaling deeply. Damp air swifts into the room, the flames lengthen back and up, and sway to the side, and then steady again, settle down.

# GREAT ROOM

# THE WOMEN

**Rachel's sorry about** Luke, sick sorry. She's very sorry for anyone who dies and especially for someone young, young as herself. They can't do anything about it now. She doesn't want to lose the weekend, too. Not what it could be. She has a photo from the passage that is unbelievable, and there's more to be had in this house. She hates herself for the thoughts of continuing any activity when a man has died. Damn the thoughts. She strikes her cheek lightly, a minor correction her mother might have done. Stop being so self-absorbed, Rachel tells herself.

"We didn't count on this," she says aloud. "I didn't cause it. We didn't."

A sound begins, like the radiators coming on again, but it's not from inside the house. It is the ticking of ice slivers nailing the night around them. The lamps go out.

"I knew it!" Deborah says.

A strange light fills the room, moonlight through iced glass, shadow world.

"Lights out everywhere at once. Lines have fallen." Rachel looks to Melody. "Leaving early wouldn't have stopped him getting hurt."

"It doesn't matter now. We can't undo anything. Let's just get this right. Let's treat him right. It won't keep us from getting out of here. The ice is doing that. He was trying to help us."

"You don't know that for sure. He may have been trying to reach a safe place for himself. He may have gone off the road."

"No matter to me. I'm going to give him the best thought possible." Melody grips the nearest corners of the quilt beneath him. "Let's move him where we're not chattering over him."

Kerosene lamps and candles glow circles in the great room, leave the illusion of tunnels where the light doesn't fall. The women pull the body across the floor, by the staircase to the hallway behind it, and into the room they call office. When they pass the staircase, Shelley places herself nearest to it, shielding them. Something is in there. Something sad and worse than sad. She wants all pain to cease and if she opens herself to all the others and to what's in the house, she might be completely swept away by their presence and lose her own. She must risk it. "We must stay together," she says, and comes near Melody, whose company is most comforting. "We should take turns sleeping, too. One of us should know what's happening every minute."

"The worst has already happened," Rachel says. "I'm sure we'll all be awake most of the night." She takes Deborah's camcorder from the round table. "Do you mind if I use this?" She fiddles with it, positions it on the mantle, pointed into the room. "I don't think my working is a disservice to Luke Essex." Holding a lamp, she goes toward the stairs, stops on the bottom step. "I plan to stay alone. You gals can double up if you wish. I want to remind you that nothing has hurt us. We didn't cause anything either. It's a bad situation, granted. Melody's right that we can't undo anything, and even if we did, I believe the only difference would be that we wouldn't have a story. Let's salvage what we can."

"I think you're hard-hearted," Melody says.

"I don't disagree." Rachel resists crying because what would it show? That she has feelings and will put them on display for other people's opinion? That she's weak?

"Sorry," Melody calls after her. "I didn't mean that. I apologize."

Rachel nods her head without turning around.

Deborah is grateful she was here to help bring his body inside. While they didn't save him, they had tried and she was there. She wasn't cringing in some corner or testing the car or thinking of how to appear brave without moving a finger. Even if he was a stranger, he was worth every effort they could make.

"We should get water and coffee and whatever else we need before we go up," Connie says. "We may not have running water by morning."

"At least we'll have sunlight," Deborah says. "And we can all go home."

# ANNA

**I love Melody's** sorrow. We should grieve deeply at loss. I wish I had lifted the log. I wish I had breathed life into him. I wish I could kiss their cheeks, spread my arms like wings and shelter them as they flee from here, trusting me. Being saved.

I wonder, suddenly, if the young man is at risk, lying in here unattended and unblessed. Not even a relic placed near. I have with me the cross from my own door. I leave the women, go to the room where they left him. I unfasten the cross, kneel by him. They have drawn the quilt to overlap at his chest. I want to slip the quilt away and lay the cross over his heart. I fumble with one edge—it will not move. I hear them upstairs. The night swirls outside the windows. I thought I had gained more strength. Something thwarts me still. I lay the cross and chain near where his heart must be, and I bow my sinner's head, in shame that I can pray only in times of such great need and even then I pray in doubt.

"Lord, here is thy servant, the young man Luke, who

gave his life saving others, a gift you well know. Keep him in your loving care and grace. Amen."

I am afraid to have no protection and seek my sanctuary again. My thoughts alone fail to take me there. I must walk. I hurry through the dim passage, reminded of the women's slowness. I come up to my own broken door. I go through it, and at the window I take down the smallest cross. I take, too, the Bible by my bed, though thoughts assail me unbidden. What good has it ever done me? Did it save my boy? I read many lines aloud, threw them at what possessed him, and threw them also to the heavens.

I clutch the Bible, open the wooden box which holds the jars I have saved. One contains a substance the color of black earth laced with dark red. Turning the jar shifts the red, as though it is liquid and flows toward itself. As a young girl, helping the old mistress, I copied a description of such a substance. The most lethal poison, the scourge of God, the dread of demons, the end of the earth in unskilled hands. I assure myself that the stopper is firmly seated, then push the jar deep into a pocket in my dress. I spin around. What more? My body lies there. I look as I have always looked, yet now I question the clarity of my vision. What if my eyes fail me as do my fingers? Perhaps I would see bones if I allowed it. I go to the bed and remove my wedding ring. If anything is granted power over me, this is.

Then I rush toward the women and am immediately with them—such peace of mind, however brief. I hear their uneasiness, their voices like little birds. I am fierce for all of them. Each of them. Let me live.

This entire night, even if it lasts an eternity, I must not retreat. I must not dream. I must trek back and forth, through the rooms, the hall, watch the stairs and ceiling, must stand and listen, train these dead senses to catch the merest of hints and then? Then what? Just be there, Anna, I tell myself. Be there, strike him, hiss at him, curse him, implore him, implore God, scream John no! John no! Find a weapon to kill him. Which perhaps I have.

# *SATURDAY,*
# *NEAR MIDNIGHT*

# JOHN

**In one corner** of the room was once a little fireplace, with sand beneath bricks to stop the occasional spark from creating a small tragedy. Before it, John had stood with a soundpost he wished to dispose of, perhaps to burn. He opened the window, and the air must have been fresh to him. In the distance were treetops. They may have reminded him of something unpleasant, like the screams of a young friend, and his own amazing strength. He rubbed his fine temples, slapped his chest four times, as if in anguish. He opened the window and he laid the soundpost down in the sill's low joint, where the wind was unlikely to catch and sail it away. A bird might have taken it. A curious bird might even have found it a mile away and flown straightaway *here to become bored with the impractical piece. No. It was John. Here, he said. I am. Don't I know that impetus? I could have flicked the soundpost away. I could have ground it to powder and sprinkled it on Anna's food. I could have carved the name Elizabeth in the most miniscule letters so that one reading it intuited the name before ever deciphering it. Small does not mean less.*

*Anna the dainty. Poisoner. P-o-i-s-o-n-e-r. Each dish had its own pinch of death. She partook of all, she never ate much, little bird beak. She sipped oil, too, before eating. She was a tome of death, and if I were human, I might marvel at the small meanings she had secreted. Her plan was transparent to me, not of course to the boy who had become a man and mine. If he sickened too much, he might not eat. So, the poison had to be gentle on his sensitive palette, had to weaken him, kill him slowly. She preferred it kill me, but she had, I believe, no illusions there. Poison could not kill me. Nothing could kill me. Can kill me. I am. I am.*

*When he sickened, she nurtured him with her soft voice and with bland foods, and with a different poison, so that as his belly eased and he slept, a burning began behind his eyes, and as she treated that with soothing compresses and a cool drink, his legs grew weak. His speech slurred, cleared, his eyes blurred. His weight fell from him. After the meals, she purged her stomach, vomited up the worst of it, and took enough nourishment to outlive him. That was her simple desire. To outlive him. Or me. If she were just wise enough, crafty enough, to destroy me, then she might, at the very last, be able to save him, and to save herself. What cared I if he was lost to her in any way? I had him. Already he had done more than I could bid him to do. He was laced with madness. He could not close his eyes without scenes he wanted to see and could not quench a craving for more of the same, worse, greater, wilder, monstrous. Pinion this, pit that, snarl and snap and rip and gut and slash, slash, slash.*

*Paint little birdies. Play little tunes. Suck a split tongue.*

*She moved him to the room within the staircase, spare, big enough for a dying young man. He lay there and she brought him soup in flat dishes and spooned it to him. He may have known she was killing him. He may have slurped death. Maybe they spoke to one another's eyes. Sometimes the eyes were mine, and I opened his mouth for her and she tipped the poison in and I swallowed it for him. She would look at my eyes and then lower hers. He would die to her. She would have me. Even if she died, too. I told her so.*

*She grew more ill herself. When she cleansed him the last time, and was he foul, foul, she closed the panel, burned the rags outside, and sought the passage. I played around her ankles. I washed the way like hot smoke and could have made a flagron of her worn dress, that patch of blue. She went in the heavy door and stood peeking out as she did today, peeking and denying me. It closed. I heard the hammering, the puny nails. I could have gone in then, under the door, through it, through the window, could have roped her proud throat with that cross chain and held her high mid room till her tongue hissed her last sound. I could have. I guarded her door instead. Guard it still, or her. Guard her. Keep her I will.*

# THE WOMEN

**Though Shelley had** slept in Connie's room last night, she wants now to stay with Melody. There are many reasons, which she can't sort. She needs to stay near to her. It's the most peaceful place. Melody is warm. Motherly to the world. And there's some other draw. "I'd like to stay with Melody," she ventures, and Deborah responds, "Good. I was hoping to stay with Connie." With lamps and candles cautiously held and set here and there, they shift their belongings.

They stand together at the railing, close to one another, looking down into the filmy great room. Behind them, the cold night hangs outside the window.

Deborah, her coat buttoned to beneath the chin, hugs herself. "I feel like we're on the upper deck of a ship and everything below has already gone beneath water."

"The worst of it is over and we're still afloat." Rachel sees Connie glance down the hall, beyond which lies the secret room. More has happened than Deborah knows. "Our position here has changed. We have a greater responsibility."

"To each other and to this place," Melody says.

"Right."

"Good night." Connie turns toward her bedroom and Deborah follows. Shelley and Melody head for the left wing; Rachel along the right hall to the room she considers hers.

Deborah can't sit down. Connie has withdrawn to the bathroom, and Deborah stands in the middle of the larger room. Her fingers reassure her that the holy water is available. She opens the green vial and dabs a bit on her forehead and wrists. She wants to put a dot of it on her tongue, like a kind of church service. Would that be sacrilegious? She isn't Catholic anyway. She moistens her finger with less than even a drop and presses that to her tongue as she might a drop of vanilla, for a sweet breath. She refastens the vial. Her own reflection in the bedroom's big window makes her uneasy, particularly because it is very bulky. She believes if she could see just a few lights on the road which is somewhere out there, way down the hill, she would feel absolutely soothed and even capable of sleeping. There are no lights. She thinks she sees a couple of black dots and steps sideways as if she's hiding behind something that is, in actuality, outside. She is then standing very close to Connie's suitcase, which is open. There she sees another vial. A blue one. She is astonished and very glad. Connie had two of them all along. She picks up the blue one, then turns and hurries out to the hall and across the landing, to the doorway of Melody's room. Shelley sits at the foot of the bed. They have a huge lighted candle and the entire middle of the room is globe shaped which makes Deborah nervous and makes her feel this moment is special. She's glad about that, too. She tenders the green vial to Shelley.

"Share this," Deborah says, "and be safe." She hurries back to her room. Already she feels something working in her. She's willing to give into it and let it fill her up however it must. It could even be the Holy Spirit. She feels terribly nostalgic and loving and lonesome. She wants Connie to get out of the bathroom. She hates being alone.

# CONNIE AND DEBORAH

**In the small** bathroom, Connie decides against medication and looks at her old-woman self in the mirror. She's haggard, and she should be. What they've been through in the last couple hours has more magnitude than her whole life thus far. That young beautiful man, his whole every chance wiped out because she and the others had come. She couldn't know. Horror and sorrow or whatever, it has been the richest and perhaps best part of her life. Sick, sad truth.

She still feels there's a ghost here, and that he and she have an attachment of some kind, as if she knows what he might do and he respects her knowledge. She has encouraged him. What if he does act? What if he does hurt one of them? Will that guilt fall on her? If he brings her down, hasn't she chosen to die that way, the stuff of story and tale, and fear? And romance, too. She wishes the love note had been in this room, not Rachel's. She wishes it had been addressed, "Constance." Of course, it would be in Rachel's room. Or Deborah's. Not hers or Shelley's or

Melody's. They are the laborers, the silent foundation under all the wonder the others so casually enjoy.

Women always want the demon lover, don't they? She is not unique. She is the poor ugly one, hoping for at least horror. Did desire have to diminish along with self-worth? Why was there no justice, no equality of happiness? Why wasn't pettiness squashed? Even her own.

She wishes she had written a book that created justice for the minions of the world, a work of art that evened the playing field for the everyday people who had doors shut in their faces before a final farewell was spoken, who had a parking place taken, who got put on hold and forgotten, who filled out forms for a refund and had it refused. And so on. Small pains were pain. Perhaps she should have been an evil person. Perhaps life would have been richer. She could have pulled the trigger and watched a face explode. Could have stared down a mean-mouthed person and then wielded the knife into the throat that voiced the words. She could only think such thoughts in abstract. Her mind rejected gore depicted. And abstract justice was not justice.

She goes into the bedroom, is glad Deborah is already under the covers, wearing her coat, odd woman, and with a pillow halfway over her head. The stock of horror films, where the monster is hiding his features and the woman is dead in the closet. She sits on the bed and, feeling ludicrous for doing so, leans to see that it is Deborah's face under there, her pretty face, too contorted to be asleep.

She stretches her back, sighs, and the hat tree gradually comes into focus, more real than her thoughts. Shelley has come to the doorway.

"I want to tell you and Deborah," Shelley says, "that the hat tree rotates, probably twice a day. I think it happens from balance alone. If you move the hats, you may throw it off schedule."

"It moves? You've seen it move?"

"No, I haven't. I've seen the hats in a different position, the arms, too. The hats don't go from one spot to another, but the arm itself is in a different position. The tree turns. That can happen just from balance. It doesn't have to scare you."

"Thanks, Shelley. I haven't seen it happening here. I trust you."

"It could frighten you if you hadn't figured it out."

"Yes, it could."

Shelley wants to say more. The urge shows in her repeated glances at Connie. She simply nods, says, "Good night," and goes away.

Connie slips between the sheets, pulls the blanket and quilts up beneath her breasts.

She has slept with six men, only one of them more than once. He was a dear friend. Even so, he had to manipulate himself to climax. She was not enough. Surely, for some men, simply thinking of the female would be enough. She didn't inspire ardor or quench it. She squelched it. The breath of her being was annihilation to desire.

She starts to extinguish the lantern, stops because Deborah is trying to turn toward her and finally manages it.

"Take that coat off," Connie says. "You can't get any rest like that."

Deborah obeys, puts the coat at the foot of her bedside. "What does holy water do?" she asks. "How does it work? Can it protect you even if you don't believe in it?"

"I don't know." Connie raises up on one elbow. "Do you want it now? Would that ease your mind?"

"No. I don't need it now. I just wondered. I believe in it more than I doubt. I want to believe it."

"It's supposed to contain the power of God and Christ. It's blessed by a priest. Nothing evil can endure the touch of it. It drives evil spirits out. It puts the sign of good on a person or thing so that evil can't enter or abide. You see, the devil can't abide long anyhow. He can enter a person through a weakness, but he can't live there permanently unless the person, the host, allows it. The will has to be involved. Some people believe he can enter only through overt, direct invitation, at the very least by employing witchcraft or magic or studying them."

"Like séances and Ouija boards."

"Yes."

"And ghost hunting?"

"I see what you're getting at. I don't think we've crossed any lines. If we have, we may also have the means to save us. The holy water. Let me get it."

"No. Not now. I'm fine."

# MELODY AND SHELLEY

**The room is cool,** dark, intimate, too, protective. Rounded strips of molding edge the ceiling, meet at carved blocks in each corner. On the bed, Melody and Shelley talk lowly and listen for the sounds of the other women and hear the murmur of voices, hear a few steps against the hall carpet runner. From outside, and above, occasional swishes mark the slide of ice and from a distance come faint cracks. There is no rare sound or sudden one. The house is a house. Melody combs through her hair with her fingers alone and begins braiding it. Shelley thinks the scene very beautiful.

"Are you wearing perfume?" Shelley asks.

"No. I keep a sachet in with my clothing."

"It's nice."

"It's the candle."

Shelley, at the foot of the bed, can see the stairs. Something may happen there.

She likes Melody very much. Rachel, too. All of them. Connie. She feels she must choose, take a part, stay with each of them, or with none. She sits up to sip a bit of water. The vial Deborah left is at her fingertips. She and Melody have already touched a drop on each other's forehead. When Melody's head is tilted away, Shelley puts a few drops into her water and into Melody's coffee. She wants Melody to be safe from everything and she doesn't want to give to Melody what she herself would not take. "We should give this holy water to Rachel now," she says.

"You're right. You want to take it down there?"

Shelley goes first to Connie's to tell her about the hat tree. She almost asks if she could stay with them, which would leave Melody alone. She hurries toward Rachel's room.

Melody feels heavy with loss and guilt. She sees again Luke's body under the branch, the shadows, hears the women's voices blurring. She hurts for him and hurts in general. There's a knot up under her left rib cage, something crowding her heart. It's a nuisance. She has to arch her back to breathe easily, and she coughs to free whatever muscle has clenched up. She may have injured herself when she lifted that branch. She remembers the belief that they were saving him, has to relinquish it again, and quickly thinks elsewhere.

Shelley is a dear. Her shyness is almost a sickness—childlike, yet not. Melody thinks that some women are lesbians without knowing it. Probably not Shelley. Connie might be, because Connie has a roughness to her, and seems mannish. Melody herself loves men and has been drawn to many of them. She married her husband because he was lusty, a strong suitor, was from an old family with good ties, and especially because he was a big man. She respects physical strength and power. When she enters gatherings with her husband, he commands the scene because he is six feet six inches, a block of a big man. He would be a leader in any age, any country. Not brilliant, he is smart enough, shrewd. They do all right together. She wishes he were here. She doesn't feel personally in danger, just very weary, and men have more strength. Women more endurance. For whatever reason, she wishes he was here.

She sips some of the tepid coffee, and, just as Shelley comes back into the room, remembers the song that had eluded her.

"Rachel wouldn't use the holy water," Shelley says. "I wouldn't take it back."

"I remembered the song about the blind girl."

"Sing it to me."

"I don't have a very pretty voice."

"You can just speak it to me."

"I'll try singing it."

*Mercy Baldwin heard a knocking, knocking,*

*heard it calling at the window,*

*the wind oh, the wind oh.*

*Mercy Baldwin heard a knocking,*

*ran she quick the windows locking,*

*for she knew who was a-knocking,*

*at her blind girl's window.*

*Not the wind, no, not the wind, no.*


"You sing beautifully," Shelley says. "I don't like the lyrics."

"They're pretty clear, aren't they? She knew her killer." Melody turns back the covers. "Are you going to sleep in your clothes?"

"Yes. I often do. It's not just here."

"It's all right with me."

Melody plumps up her pillow, gets in bed in the space allowed, trying to raise her legs without much pressure on her stomach. "We'll go home tomorrow. There's no sense in staying. We'll go. Don't you worry." She lies back, watching Shelley who nods but stares ahead. "If we're in danger, Shelley, you should tell us. Even if you just think we are."

Shelley bows her head. "We are. I don't know from what. I don't trust myself."

"I trust you."

# RACHEL

**Rachel has a** journal propped against her leg, and though the candlelight is too feeble for the words to be legible, she writes straight and firmly, controlling her script. She is logging the day's events, all the while aware that except for the photo and death, they could have been fabricated. The death couldn't have been foreseen. Now it has happened, and everything she and the others have done up to and after the death is of greater importance. The death elevates the whole experience, makes it rarer, a real story. She hadn't asked for that, wouldn't have wished a death. She can't help that it has occurred. She doesn't have to deny it. It is a macabre gift.

The candle on her nightstand flickers and little lights float away from it. When she closes her eyes briefly, she sees flickers inside her eyelids. She remembers the black dots in Deborah's camcorder shots. She looks up at the short, wide windows, and around the room. In candlelight, the remaining darkness is wavery, floating layers. If a fire began, and her door slammed shut, as happens in movies, she'd burn up alive. She'd never get out of these windows. They are likely the kind that don't open. They are to look through, not open out or in. *Burn in hell old Rachel*, she thinks, and the thought horrifies her, as if it just landed there, wasn't hers at all. As if God spoke to her in her own language.

She sits up, takes the camera from the nightstand. She doesn't look at the photo she took in the passage. She just wants to hold the camera, and to have it in bed with her. Is there any way the photo could have been a setup? Images could have been painted along the walls, she supposed, light-sensitive images? Like blood could show up if a particular chemical was sprayed on it. It could show up even after years. Even after a scrubbing with bleach. Maybe images had been prepared at different locations along the walls, continuous, like a mural, and pranksters knew about the tunnel mural all along, part of the house's legend. Like a pictorial diary. Like the opposite of the timeline of murder.

She is scaring herself.

From the beginning then—except for the death, everything could have been prepared for their entertainment. People knew they were coming here. Husbands and friends. Possibly historical society volunteers, merchants, and realtors. The thought of her husband, Joe, brings a twinge of heartache. He'd never pull a mean stunt on anyone. Luke, though, could have been in on it and got caught in his own mischief. A true accident. She is really, really sorry. She chokes and cries a little. She's tired. Go on. Go on. Luke Essex. All right. According to Melody, he was an entertainer by nature. His whole family was. He had probably been rigging the boiler to shut off when Melody saw him leaving the cellar. The old newspapers—anyone connecting the murders would think the bastard had lived—and killed during—an impossible span of years. That was the very purpose of the newspapers, to hint that a murderer who lived that long possibly still lived. Had never died. The handwritten, linear chart of murders committed, names of towns, dates, even a few penciled-in victims' names, was intended to match something else they were meant to find. More newspapers or photos, maybe another body. And as for the attic, that woman. She could be fake. Wax figures alone were remarkably lifelike, and given the techniques today, could probably fool a relative. No human body could have been that preserved. The ink was proof positive. It couldn't have lasted for over a hundred years. It would have dried up. It had been provided so a note could be left. First a hint of a note, and then a completed one, which she and the others were probably to have found on the next visit to the attic.

Luke's death had stopped the charade. Whoever had been setting them up couldn't pull the rest of their stunts because reality had upstaged them. The death had turned things around, too. It was the kind of thing that makes a story. No one asked for it. There was no shame in taking advantage of it.

The candle sputters. The room is a sea of murky shadows. She feels as if she might float from the bed and be lost. When she was a child, she called on the saints to preserve her, though she wasn't a Catholic — Catholics were, in fact, spawn of the Whore of Babylon, the Catholic church, mentioned in Revelations. She was innocent as a child, and safe. Always safe. She had rituals — *Matthew, Mark, Luke and John, bless this bed I lie upon. Now I lay me down to sleep, I pray the Lord my soul to keep.* No more innocent. No more child. No more hypocrite.

Another memory.

*Black Bobby calls my name at night from where the plaster's cracked.*

*If ever I invite him in, he's never going back.*

She relights the candle which prefers, apparently, to drown in the wax. She tilts the candle enough for wax to run down the stem without dripping.

She holds the camera against her stomach. But this. The photo she took in the tunnel. What is it?

She swallows any possibility of crying. Nothing's ever definite. She wants to know this being is *real*. Just *is*. She's tired of coming to a belief all by herself and having it not be one that grants her safety or freedom from who she is. She has to fashion the what with no why or how.

She's going to take all the crap with her, and she's going to write a book. Not an article. A book. She decides to get the note from John to Elizabeth, compare the script with that on the sketches and the butcher paper. She opens the drawer. No note. She looks around the room, though she knows she hasn't left it on anything. Could one of the other girls have taken it? She sits on the bed, peering at her walls. She hears a slight thrashing, and wonders if someone is getting up. Silence ensues and remains. She hears, too, a screech owl, odd in the ice world. And a very thin sound, like a weak voice that seems to come from outside the house, or down in the great room, nowhere up here near her and the other gals. Only a few hours more. Come on dawn. Come on daybreak.

# ANNA

**I pass through** the rooms. Rachel writes in her book, alternately inhaling from a cigarette and chewing the end of her pen. Her foot taps against the bedding. Her eyebrows draw sharply down. If she fell asleep, the bedding would blaze up in seconds. On the table in the room where Melody and Shelley whisper is a knife, slender, yellow-handled, closed. I grasp it. It will not be lifted! Why do such tiny things elude me? Must an object be mine before I can take it? Shelley has slipped from the end of the bed to stand on the floor and peer at me. Or is it the knife she stares at?

Melody has plaited her hair into a thick rope that lies across her breast. She has changed into a gown and has propped a pillow between her back and headboard. Her eyes are weary. The skin beneath them is thin, gray.

She sings a song to Shelley. It is familiar to me, though I hope not the words. I don't want to discover a life I have had without knowing and must accept as part of myself.

In my and William's room, Deborah and Connie lie

facing each other. There is a space between them wide enough for another person. Deborah whimpers.

"We'll make it, Deborah," Connie soothes. "We'll be home soon. I know you've been miserable. We should have encouraged you to go home the minute you began to feel bad. In our defense, we didn't know it was going to get worse. And now. Damn. Look at us. I am sick about Luke. He was a young guy. He should have had years. It's such a waste. I wish it'd been me instead. I'd just like to be certain that there's another life afterward. Even if there isn't, sometimes the peace of it all seems lovely. Not to hurt."

"I was feeling better. Now? After someone dying! I can't think about anything lovely. I feel churned up. I don't want to die no matter what awaits. And you shouldn't either, Connie. You're worn out from thinking about it. You need rest. Go to sleep. I'll stay awake for us both."

"There's no need for that. I want to stay awake. Keep watch."

"So do I. I want to do my part."

This is my charge. To protect them. I don't know where to wait. I stand at the railing. Below, the ice-filmed windows turn the great room wavery, as if it is both sky and ocean, night and day. I take my Bible from the table where I once placed a lamp and I think of verses to read or to tear out and tuck into the garments of each woman. I move to the very top of the stairs. Directly below it, in a narrow room, lies a body I dearly loved. My son.

I want to pray. I have words. Pleas for help. I don't want to kneel or close my eyes and trust that a heavenly strike of blade or thought will save us all. I must be fervent and sincere, inadequate in myself.

I see him coming from the side, to the lower steps. He is a young man with the same visage as John. No. He is not John. This one will hurt them. I tremble and fear floods me, weakens me, but I stay. I long to draw the heavens to me, some strength! I entreat.

"Scatter the enemy by your power."

"Defend and deliver us."

"Be our defense and refuge."

"Cast out any devil near us."

"Cleanse this house. Cleanse me, Oh Lord."

"Wipe the wicked from your creation. Oh Lord."

"Be my right hand and my left hand."

"From you comes all my strength."

"Be with me oh my Lord."

Yet he comes, as if it were long years ago when he ignored my pleading voice to tell me what he'd done. Tell me. Up the steps, slowly, watching me while seeing elsewhere, too, nowhere. Mind's eye.

"No! No! John!" I go down two steps, a third. "No! Son!" I see the yellow cravat, see the gold chain from a pocket watch that was his father's, long gone, see the tendrils of brown hair framing his face and neck, the deep brown eyes. He identifies himself as mine. He is immediately before me. Still clenching the Bible, I shove him. "Begone! Demon! Devil! Begone!" I push, push, but am driven backwards, up. "God curse you! God kill you! God seal you away forever!" I pummel him and he allows me to, waiting through my struggle. Then there is this sharp cry and he is gone. For a moment I believe he is vanquished, and I have driven him away. I hear a gasp and I am in Melody's room. Shelley struggles on the bed, striking at something dark. She cries and strikes. I know what she attempts to kill. It can't be killed. She sobs with the thrusts. I try to grab her but am held back and I slam my fists into what must be him and scream, "John No!" and I am touching Shelley, the thin arms, the shiver, the fierce force of her. She shudders into stillness, sobbing. The room is empty save us. Shelley slides from the bed, stays bent as if too weak to stand, holds onto the footboard to steady herself and stumbles toward the door, out to the landing. "Help us," she says. "Help us."

Melody lies on her side, facing the wall. Blood stains the back of her gown. She rolls a little toward me. Blood spots spread together on her bodice. Her eyes are open, only the white showing. The sheet is bloody where she has lain. She is direly wounded but breathes. Lives. For how long? He has done this, through Shelley's hands and my ineptitude. And God's acquiescence.

The others are on the landing with Shelley. The moon shines on them all. Shelley is bloody. Hands bloody. Shirt. Cheeks. She is stunned near stupor. "I tried to stop him," she mutters. "I tried." They leave her, run to help Melody. I come to Shelley who shakes with sobs. I want to kiss her. *Dear girl. Dear girl.*

# SUNDAY,
## BETWEEN MIDNIGHT AND DAWN
## JOHN

**It might be** interesting to die. I think it is not in my nature. If I have died before, I do not know of it. I think there are many of me and we are one. I do what I do, am what I am and am where I am. It is not a carrying forth or altering but an is. When I surface there is what I will do. When I am here, Anna is here, and Anna is mine. I know her, her son who is more mine than he can ever be any other. When I travel out, I encounter more I know and more I have. Rage calls me, lust calls me, loneliness calls me, despair calls me, fear, need, hardness. I have so many, many beckonings, and love them all. Love is a satisfaction, a joy, a temporary bliss. Bliss.

Anna posed her questions aloud and that mate of hers tried to answer what he didn't understand.

*He would press his lips to hers in the midst of her speaking, as if to cut off her words and her thoughts. Once she bit his lip for doing so and the bite drew blood. I would like to swallow whatever she is and have it whole inside me for whatever my future is.*

*She is at the railing now and contemplates me in her misery. I have bested her every move. I have been generous and tolerant. She is beaten and does not know it.*

# SUNDAY,
# PREDAWN

## ANNA AND THE WOMEN

**They have tended** Melody's wounds, cleaned them, bandaged them singly and with strips of cloth around her upper body. She lies on the stained sheet, two pillows propping up her head and shoulders. She eyes her suitcase, across which her brown skirt and top lie. Deborah, who has been guarding her, has left briefly to learn what next is planned. Melody slides her legs to the edge of the bed, over, down, and stands. Whatever the others do, she's doing. Breathing shallowly, she gathers the skirt and blouse in hand, but she can't quite reach the bed again. It breaks her fall. She drops the clothing and fumbles, slowly, fully onto the bed. She rests a few seconds, then attains the pillow and turns onto her back.

In the big bedroom, Connie and Rachel have scrubbed Shelley till her skin is raw pink and the hair close to her face damp and springy. Dazed, she appears eased by their nearness and attention. The three sit on the bed. A crystal night lies beyond the window. A lantern is by the bed and a weaker light flutters in the small room off the bedroom. It is where William's clothing used to be stored, ironed and folded by me in the best manner I knew. Now I see they have there a sink, and a mirror, and porcelain toilet bowl. I wish sorely to step forward and face myself in that mirror. To know what I am, have become. What if I am not who I believe myself to be? I see, near my waist, my hands. They are as always. I thrust one hand into the room before the mirror and lean to see no true image, only a blur, as if the glass steams over. I step into the room wholly. The wide mirror should show my features, black hair, wide, thin shoulders, a blue dress with pink sprigs, deep cuffs and band collar. William's favorite. I am no more than air and a wish. I am a longing vapor. They can't see me. I can't see myself. The sink bears pinkish streaks. Shelley's clothing lies crumpled on the floor. I can grip the shirt but cannot lift it. What good am I?

"The key will be in Luke's pocket." Connie says. "He may have left the truck on the highway below. It could be stuck somewhere coming up here, though. If we have the key and the truck's movable, we can get help faster. We'll have to be careful. One of us will need to stay with Melody."

"I'll do it," Deborah says from the doorway. "I'm afraid to, but I will."

"We'll talk about it. Right now, let's get the key. Deborah, you stay with Melody while we go downstairs."

"And if the key's not there?" Rachel asks.

"We walk out anyhow. At least, I'm going to, and I think Shelley should come with me." Getting up, Connie shudders, kneels, and rummages in her suitcase. "I can't find that vial. The holy water." She turns without rising. "I had a vial with holy water. Right here in the suitcase. I didn't take it out."

"Oh!" Deborah presses the heels of her palms to her cheeks. "I have it! I made a mistake! I saw it in your suitcase when we came up last night." She twists to extract from her coat pocket the blue vial, takes it to Connie. "I'm sorry. Sincerely sorry. I thought the other one was holy water, too. The green vial."

"Where did you see it?"

"I found it. In the kitchen yesterday."

"What did you do with it?"

"I used some. Then, when I saw this vial, I thought you had two of them. I gave the green one to Shelley. I told her to share the water with Melody. I thought I was doing a good thing."

From behind them, Rachel says, "What was in the green vial, Connie?"

"An herb. Salvia. It's mild but I brewed it down to make it stronger. I've kept it around in case I get desperate enough for an exciting moment that I would risk a little craziness, bodily craziness. I haven't used it, just read about it and procured it. It's like having a passport when you're afraid to travel. Now, I may have hurt someone. Did you drink it, Shelley? Did you drink what was in the vial?"

Shelley's blue eyes are stricken. She can't respond.

Rachel comes over, extends the green vial to Connie. "I have it. I didn't use it. Thank God." She turns to Shelley, hugs her, and says close to her ear, loud enough for the others to hear, "What did you do before Melody brought it to me? Come on, honey. Tell us. It's okay."

"I put drops in my water and in Melody's cup."

"That's it, then," Connie declares. "It could have thrown her," she nods at Shelley, "into another state. That's what it's supposed to do. Not for long and not a wild state, just an altered one. It's supposed to be harmless." To Deborah, "I'd like to say you did this. You caused it all. But I brought the stuff, didn't I? I lost the vial, too, and didn't say a word. I thought it was outside, on the ground. It wasn't worth worrying about, not with everything that happened." She brushes back the curls around Shelley's face. "You won't get in trouble for this. I'll see to it." She glances at the hallway door. "I don't know what to do. I'll just get started. First, I want to get some of the holy water on each of you, especially Shelley, and then I plan to burn her clothes. And get rid of that knife."

"Don't burn my clothes." Shelley darts toward the bathroom, turns to face Connie. "I didn't do it. Don't burn my clothes. His blood will be on them. Or something of him will be on them. You'll make me guilty by hiding."

"It's Melody's blood, hon," Rachel soothes. "I'm sorry, you did stab her. She's the wounded one."

"She cried out and was sitting up, holding her chest, like this," Shelley draws her fists up together, tight between her breasts. "A man was by the bed, and he had the knife. He had it. Not me. I grabbed it from him and I hit him with the knife. I hit him hard. I couldn't hurt him. He grabbed me close and maybe then I hit Melody. I don't think so. I hit *him*."

"You hit Melody, Shelley. Not a man." Rachel speaks to Connie and Deborah. "Her fingerprints are going to be all over the knife. On Melody too."

"I didn't do it!" Shelley moans. "I told you. I would know. I wouldn't lie to you."

"You had blood all over you, Shelley. We all saw it. No man was there. Only you and Melody."

"It's *his* blood. He was hurting her. I wasn't! He just left. I was there. Melody was hurt. I went for help. I went for *you*."

"Okay. Okay. We'll leave your clothes. Deborah will stay up here with Melody. The rest of us will go down for the key. Getting to the truck is the hard part."

"Two of us should stay here with Melody."

"No. Two have to be with Shelley, just in case."

"I didn't do it." She slumps. "Truly. I didn't. I wouldn't."

Downstairs smells like ashes. They stoke the fire and Rachel adds a new log. She has brought her bag down and empties it onto a chair and begins to place the box contents into the bag — sketches, photos, newspapers.

"You're going to carry that out when we leave?" Connie asks.

"I don't see any reason not to. The weekend's over, I agree. We need to get help for Melody and for Shelley. There's no need for me to lose my notes and everything."

"Only the notes are yours. Those items belong to the owner of the house. Besides, we'll have to come back with the police. You could get the stuff then."

"I think I'd better take it while I have a chance. They're going to demand we relinquish everything. We may never see it again." She suddenly stares at the mantel. "I forgot! The camcorder!"

She hurries to the fireplace, takes the instrument down, opens it. She glances quickly at the stairs, then around the room as if someone lurks there. "Look at this," she whispers. "Look at this." Connie is by her immediately.

Questions burst from Rachel. "Where did the guy go? Did he go in Melody's room? Was there time for him to have been in the room as Shelley said? What was that cry?

Was something with him on the landing, that second or so? What was that?" She reaches for Shelley. "Come here," she says gently. "Can you tell if this is the man you saw?"

Shelley doesn't move. Rachel takes the instrument to her. "Is it?"

"I don't know."

"If Shelley didn't do it," Connie says, "then he did. He can hurt us, too."

"Not if we're alert. Shelley was changed. She had that stuff in her. And something scared her. Maybe Melody did. We're warned. We're watching each other. He can't physically do anything. He makes someone else do it."

"He was physically in the room with them," Connie says. "I believe Shelley. He appeared real. What if there's more than one of him? Hordes of them?" She raises the blue vial. "Here. Let me put . . ."

"No."

"Why are you afraid of the holy water, Rachel? It's such a little thing to do."

"I'm not afraid of it. I made my choice. If there's help around us, then let it act without a petty ritual. I don't want to beg and shouldn't have to. None of us should."

# SUNDAY,
# PREDAWN,
# OUTDOORS

## ANNA AND THE WOMEN

**I see the** video as they do. They have him, almost at the top of the stairs, like a real man, a living being, his head back and to the side as if dodging something and his arms open wide. He has taken an image to use. My son. Where am I? It is only he and a faint whiteness, as if the moon fell bright into a mirror. Nothing of substance there to hold him back. Where is my voice? Where are my prayers? My blows? He doesn't advance, though. Then comes again that quick high cry — and he's gone. So is the light. Then muffled sounds, only that, and someone approaches. Shelley. Bloody. Dazed.

I know the answer to Rachel's question. Yes, it's the man Shelley saw, and I saw. And I know the cry came first. Someone was in distress *before* he left me. That was his cue! He was ready for that, exactly that. Melody had clutched her chest, Shelley said. She had cried in pain and he answered. He knew it would happen. He gave Shelley an illusion to strike. The false body of an attacker. Her blows in defense fell through him and into Melody. I didn't move quickly enough. What could I have done? What more can he do that I must watch?

I don't know his basic form. He can display beauty in the form of Luke, of John. Perhaps of others. I study our small group. He can't, I believe, be two places at once. We have each been separated from the others. He could have had access to any of us. Rachel was upstairs first and in the room with the newspapers. Deborah was outside many times, longing to leave. She gave the vial to Shelley and Melody. Now, strangely, she has ceased her complaining.

Something nags me, so obvious that I fear I've been a fool. The caretaker? Whom John has perhaps seen before and could mimic? How we struggled to bring him in, how we excited ourselves and our fears and our hearts. How the death defeated us all. All this grief and despair pouring into the air, especially from Shelley, who is tautly strung, having to curb herself to live in peace. What being did we tend? Why could I not place the cross close to the heart? I must know. I don't dare leave them alone even seconds.

"We should look at the body," I announce. "We should together look at the body. It may not be the caretaker." Shelley stirs. She is watching where I am, even if she doesn't see me. I stand directly before her. "Shelley, dear, we will take care of you. We must all go look at the body. All of us at once. No one left alone." She has found my thought. She stands. I touch her shoulder before she steps away. "Not alone! Shelley!"

"We should check the body," she says aloud.

"Why?" from Rachel.

"To see if he's there."

Exactly. They understand her meaning. They gather themselves up.

"He was dead," Connie says, doubt tinging her words.

Silver clings to the windows, sheens the outer room. The fire winks and clicks. The clock chimes four times. One of them must have wound it.

"Shelley's right," Rachel says. "I think we should check."

They stay close together, and I behind them.

"Oh Jesus," I hear—Rachel's voice. I know before I am able to see around them that the body is gone. The quilt, folded, lies where the body had lain, like a present, the cross on top.

They are stunned. We are stunned, though I shouldn't be. I should have known. I have been so hungry to win somehow. To remedy. Now.

"He couldn't have left on his own," Connie says. "Even if he wasn't dead. He was injured badly."

"Maybe not. Like you said, the cold could have protected him somehow. He woke. He went to get help."

"He would have called for us."

"Maybe he just managed to get up and out and that was the best he could do."

"Look at the quilt. Look. Would he have folded it?"

"Let me think. Let's get in front of the fire. We should get Deborah and Melody down here with us."

"Wait." Connie says. "If it wasn't Luke, if he didn't go for help, then who was he? What was he?"

"Not a ghost," Shelley says.

"No," Connie says. "I agree. So, Rachel, we don't know what he can do. We have to get all of us out of here now. We may not be able to make it but that's our best chance."

"What makes it safer out there on the ice in the middle of the night instead of here, where we have some kind of heat? We can stay awake, stay in a circle right here, wait till morning."

"Or two of us can go for help now. Shelley and I can go."

Rachel stares at the fire. "We have to use our heads. We can't run wildly. Think. He can't *hurt* us. It's true. He *hasn't* hurt us. We can hurt each other. He can play games and scare us and trick us. He can't physically hurt us. Do you see that? Don't panic. I have to tell you, I thought there was something in the house that would help us. I have some evidence of that."

"What help?" from Connie. "What evidence?"

"Her," a glance upward. "The woman we saw. She hasn't helped us. Maybe she can't."

Now it falls to me more heavily than ever. Rachel has expected something of me, a little web of safety. I've failed. And now they'll leave the house, to go where I cannot. He's the roamer. I have no choice about how far I go. I'm made a certain way, as they are. I can't finish myself. They begin turning away, I bend and grab the cross that was mine. There's no aversion to it in my body, no fear of it. That is the only test I have of my nature. I will wear it even with no faith in it or in myself.

For so long I've hidden in memories, fled to them. I don't know how to go into the world. How will I get back? If I thought William awaited me, I would dare the journey. But to leave here, where he might return, and risk losing my son and what is left of me, is more than I can do. I prefer to dream. I prefer to be in the sanctuary, sealed away forever, behind small windows and fake facades. Dream.

Is this a trick? Could one of the guests have left the folded quilt as a sign? A woman's touch? Connie? Rachel? Shelley? Has he already taken possession of one of them?

Rachel will take that bag. She is vehement against Connie's request. She will not leave it. It is evidence.

"We're using the holy water," Connie says. "We have to."

"Not for me." Rachel steps away as Connie applies a drop of water to Shelley's forehead.

"Then something may be wrong with you," Connie says. "How can we follow you without knowing? Do this."

"No. I'm not afraid to walk out alone either. He's all pretense. He has no true power over us."

I want Connie to apply the water to me, but I have no right, even now. I choose to be their protector. They're not mine.

"Are you leaving?" Deborah calls from the top of the stairs. "Be safe."

Connie, foot already on the lower step, speaks over her shoulder. "Rachel, you'll have to get them out. I'm going to stay here." She starts up. "Deborah, come down. I want to stay. It has to be me." Subduing her desire to be in the fore, Connie continues upward, beckoning Deborah. "I'm too old and worn out to make the trip," she says. "Really. I couldn't make it. I'd jeopardize you. I'll stay by Melody. You go." They pass on the stairs and Deborah, momentarily of a height with Connie, leans so they touch cheeks.

We exit through the kitchen and mudroom into the side yard. Rachel takes the lead, Shelley behind her, and Deborah in front of me. The bag Rachel carries by a strap over one shoulder is as long as her torso and she sways to keep balance.

We go out into the night. I hear the crunching of their steps, hear their breathing, small sounds as they slip and right themselves.

We go past their vehicle. Rachel stops, turns around. "You have the car keys, Deb? Give them to me."

Deborah obeys. "It's not going to start now."

"We need it. It'll start."

Rachel goes to the vehicle, jerks the door. It doesn't open. She tries again, then kicks the car and curses. She turns toward us. "Who's with you?" she asks. "Who is that?" She sees something that Deborah and Shelley don't. And neither do I. "Help me," she says, and sags down. Deborah runs to grab her arm, twists to see what torments Rachel.

"Together," Shelley cries, and runs toward them. "We have to move all at once together. Don't separate. Touch."

They walk away from the car, clustered close. Rachel shifts the bag to her right shoulder and side, on the outside of their group. I am alone, behind them, separate though I don't wish to be.

The ice reflects the moonlight, keeps the black firmament high, holds the stars distant like millions of spectators, fruitless angels. We are paltry against so vast a screen.

"His truck!" Deborah points. "That's the caretaker's truck down there, isn't it?"

A few yards on, something colorful lies just off the road. Colors like those we carried into the house. Luke. His lanky body is unmoving but his hand is up and open. Maybe frozen that way.

"It's him," Deborah cries. "Is he alive?"

"Don't stop," Shelley says. "We don't know who he is."

Rachel whimpers, a foreign sound from her. "Oh, I can't bear it. What is it? What is it?"

"Rachel," I say. "Rachel." I come up beside her. "Rachel!" She's like a mechanical doll, color and expression leached from her face. "Let me help her," I plead. "Let me!" I touch her. I feel the sharp cold, the cleansing of it, immediately replaced by a foulness in my throat, my breasts, my bowels, my mind, like tendrils of scorn.

She drops to her knees. The others bend and kneel by her. "What is it, Rachel?"

"He's here," Shelley says. "Don't look at him."

`A film draws together from the night, the translucent becoming dense enough for sight, forming beside us. I want not to look, believing I might recognize the beauty, the kinship with each of us, might see someone I love. I fear he may not appear as my son, but as my William, and I will have committed the worst of errors in the name of goodness. He turns as if he wants to grant me this, and I see him. I look at him, fully.

So beautiful. I am drawn toward the glorious creature.

He doesn't touch the earth with us, doesn't breathe the air, lives otherwise. Fair. Tall and muscular. Arrogant. Haughty eyes, black eyebrows and black, flowing, thick hair, a sensuous mouth, aquiline nose, square jaw. Kinglike and beastlike in the fervent boldness of his gaze on us each, sweeping over us with ownership and something not hate, not love. A want. I break away, return with quick glimpses.

Is this truly his form? Or is it, too, mimicry, the sheen of great beauty over whatever he is, swelling, pulsing. The eyes, oh. Black. Flat. Nothing human. I look again, directly, and quickly away. A vast, fireless want. The cold slides over us, settling on Rachel. He locks on her, where she kneels in the ice.

"No," I say. "No."

"Anoint her," Shelley tells Deborah. "Hurry."

I try to think myself above them, above him too, above them and vaporous, wide, so I might shield them away from him, enwrap them in whatever I can be and move them bodily to safety.

Ripples of sound come over us, their names, repeated.

"He knows us," Deborah cries. "He said my name. It's too late. We can't get away."

"Allow me," I pray to the sky. "Please, allow me."

I am staggered by the onslaught, by the burning grief in my mind, the unrelenting foreverness of it, the desire to squelch it, destroy it, escape, and all the while it grows. This is what Rachel feels.

Deborah moistens her fingertips with drops from the blue vial, rubs them into Rachel's temples. "You're safe, Rachel. Safe. Believe it. We're here. You're not alone. He doesn't have you. We have you." She embraces the fallen Rachel.

"Don't think on him," Shelley says to the others. "Deny him. Think of one another only. Close. Think close."

She is right. Together.

Shelley takes the vial from Deborah. She empties it into her palms. Instead of applying it to her own flesh, she turns toward me, as if she sees me. She holds her hands out and I understand. It is for me. It is for me among them. To help. It is most sweet. I bury my face in those small palms. I kiss them. "God love you," I say.

Little wondrous creature she is. Made so but also by choice.

Deborah is in the fore and Shelley and Rachel behind. Rachel has kept the bag. That is her weakness. And now ours. I must be more than I am, must be above them.

He speaks to me, *Anna, Anna.* I have this thing to do that I have learned. To be around them. Just that. To separate from harm for as long as I can.

We near the bridge which was treacherous in my time and remains so. The boards clatter as Rachel and Deborah step on them. I can go no further. I cannot go. Please, I beg the stars. Let me finish this. Please. I fall back, and fade, not from place, but from force.

"Help them" I cry. "Help them."

At the fence near the road appears the old man who wanders these grounds. He clambers over it, raises the wire for his yellow dog to come beneath. I don't know what good he can do, if he has any powers at all. He falls into step behind them. They do not see him. I want to be with them. I want to follow that road I once followed. I want life again, my home, my son, myself. The real sun, real snow. I want to be part of their salvation.

He takes form again, the one I know. My son's face and bearing. He is not following them, though others may be. He is attuned to me, by will or nature.

I think how to help them now, and I seek the small, old jar in my pocket. They must survive. They must see that my son is buried and allowed to leave this plane. I must do away with that which has bonded with him. The dawn will come, the ice will melt, and everything beneath it will be dead only not yet appear so. When summer comes, the trees will show only bones, and jagged limbs. Creatures will be bewildered and search for other havens.

I know where I must go. I hurry, because he studies me. Don't I feel that prying eye.

I am in the cellar, where he slithered out in whatever

form he had. Perhaps he has gone back and out many times. Perhaps he has slain women while he was in the body of one crazed, miserable creature after another. Perhaps I have even heard screams and have hidden in my limbo of want and desire, want for my husband, my child, my past, my life. Now here I stand over this simple structure that someone fashioned. I bend over the pipe, listen. What is he, that took my son. How many of him? .Do I hear their very nature in that dull roar? Do they wait? I take the jar of poison from the fold pocket of my blue dress. Holding it firmly, I position it so the tiny, rounded opening, when the stopper is removed, will be directly over the pipe's mouth. If I could wait until just as I hear the women returning, know that they have succeeded, have survived, and will find my son and bury him properly, then the moment would be perfect. As that assurance arrived, I would eradicate the being that has blended with my son. Eradicate him and his kind. Purge them from the bowels of the earth. No matter if others live in other spaces, weave throughout the fabric of the universe, no matter. I will have destroyed these. They will breed no more in this underground, will travel no more where I stand.

He appears, and I dare not wait. He is my son now. That face, known well by me. He is taller, attempting command, with a falsely courteous, shallow bow.

"What do you have there, Anna?" he asks, speaking

not as my son. "Is it a gift for the whole world?"

His words give me pause. He repeats.

"For the whole world, Anna?"

He has raised the doubt. Would I destroy only his kind or others, too? The whole world of other creatures who just want to live with only the normal miseries of life to struggle against, not those seized upon and magnified by his kind. I doubt. I would not wish to cause others more grief, or to take away from them the glory of spring, and sun, and wind, and winter, and the smell of fresh grass, and the sight of a baby, of a loved husband, of the touch of a human, of a creature like oneself.

I doubt. I stopper the jar and return it to my pocket. It is mine not to use.

"Good girl," he says.

What I feel is hate.

# SUNDAY,
# PREDAWN

# JOHN

*Evil isn't malevolent, isn't intentional, only ready. Something happens and evil rises to the occasion. Evil is much like a virus, say, or a parasite, a tick that lies in a dry crack in the wall for years, or in the dirt beneath dead grass, and then — some living and blooded creature comes near. Another nature rallies, expends great effort, even if it's toward death, to act as meant to act, to survive as meant to survive. One being weakens or dies, another lives and thrives. No malevolence there. Fulfilling the created intent. Ready to the occasion.*

*They have each invited me. I do not pursue. I am. Am. Here and there. I smell the whole earth, some pulses warmer than others. Some eyes brighter. I can go everywhere.*

*I cannot abide everywhere. I have no form of my own.*

*Is there a great master to whom I bow in ugly fashion? No. Is there a great master who himself will not bow. I don't know. I did not design the world or design myself. I act. I am. Is this living? It is being. Being. Evil is but a word. Good is but a word. God is but a word. Anna's word.*

*A Mary Bledsoe bled so. I had no part in that. She bought an elixir from a charlatan and thinking to cure her daughters, thinned her family's ranks instead. She then cured herself in the same fashion. A Jennifer crossed a field on a windy day and a bull, by no other name, no other nature, gored her youth to a standstill. Evil? No. Simply done by a power greater than mine.*

*There was a house, though, with a sweet bird inside, who trilled like a lark. There was also a man who watched her from his window, and his yard, and who stood in the woods and watched her portal as though it would open for him. She sometimes cleaned his home, groping beautifully. Blind girl. He watched. I watched. His portal opened for me, and I opened hers for him. Sweet, sweet. He died by his own hand, and I came back to my own place. Here.*

*That was Deborah's story. The blind girl.*

*I like to tell the stories. I like to hear them. Always there are details delayed, lost, or destroyed.*

# SUNDAY, DAWN

## ANNA

**I open the** panel to the staircase room. That is not truly John. John was and is no more. Not for me. I must know that in my heart. I sit in the cane chair by the narrow bed. No more than bones and hair and rags is he now. I wanted to save my son and damn whatever had him. And if there was such a thing as a soul, I wanted, at whatever cost, to save John's. The little baby with the tremble cry hadn't asked to be born. He nursed at my breast because he was born to breathe, thrive, live and love, fulfill some sort of destiny. He didn't *ask* for it. He didn't create himself. God did. And William and I did. I claimed him back.

We ate together always, at either table depending on his or my mood. Along with our meals were occasionally soups, dark breads, salads, with sweetened seeds, silvers of a paler seed hidden here and there, a stem, a blossom, a mushroom. All innocent. A common pattern.

I prefer to believe it was my son who ate, whose gaze caught mine sweetly as he finished and laid his napkin across his plate as had been his father's custom.

And there he lies, not as I remember, as he is now, to them. Gone. Decayed. I would like to see him once more, as my son, fully fleshed, clean minded, full of life and hope, without the other. That is not possible. I hope to have saved his soul. I wanted always only to save him. I stand, come close to his last form. I close my eyes for a few seconds, see my son's fair face. I speak to that face as I look at the bed.

"Goodbye. Goodbye John."

I leave, out the panel, around to the steps. It doesn't know what I think. It watches to learn. It cannot be easily deceived. And something in it has to obey. There are rules for it, as there are rules on this whole world: Poison here, but cleansed thusly. Sin here, but forgiveness thusly.

I hurry to Melody and Connie. Connie has drawn a chair by the bed, facing the door. She sleeps. Her body slumps toward the mattress and her head droops. They both sleep. On the nightstand is the bloodied knife. I walk behind the chair and reach for the yellow handle. I place thumb to one side and curl my fingers around it and I think to feel it mine, against my palm, closed in. I have it. I can hear Connie's breathing. I know the other is nearby, perhaps in the hallway, watching me. I might see him if I tried. I allow him no part of my act. I dwell on my movement, my goal, hold the knife firmly and hurry down the stairs to the kitchen. I scrub the knife with water and soap and brush. I clean it, clean it. Dry it. He is by the counter, as my son.

"You are blaming the wrong person as always," he says. "I harmed no one. Why do you blame me? Punish me? You know who truly bears the blame. Mother."

I cry without sound. He tricks me.

"Where did William go that day?" he asks. "Would you know? Be certain? I can tell you."

I run up the stairs with the knife, run down the hall, past my son's empty room, through the wall, up the steps into my broken sanctuary. I take the piece of white linen that had lain beneath the Bible near my bed, and with the knife split the fabric at two sides. I fold the blade into the handle, wrap the cloth around the knife and tie the cut strips. I slip it thusly wrapped into a pocket of my dress. The object is mine, as I am, hidden as long as I am hidden.

He is at the portal. I sense his presence more real than the presence of God, though I long for the latter to be near. I sit at my desk and while I write what I must, I whisper the words aloud, too. I hear them. Perhaps God does. When I finish, I dip the fingers of my right hand one by one into the inkwell, then press them against the paper. I am affixing the seal of Anna.

Sun lightens the window. A day lives outside and I

forever here? He has not entered. Is that God's power or the weakness of evil? How can I know? *My son, I give you up again. I give you up to wherever it is that you must go. With all my love and hope that you fare well.* At the door, I kneel down to where the broken space is widest. He is there.

# SUNDAY,
# DAWN

# JOHN

**Her hands are** *stained. She doesn't raise her face to meet my gaze. She fears me yet. Good. So she should, though I would do her no harm. She speaks to the patch of wood between us.*

*"I have confessed to what my son may have done in his time and since. I have accepted responsibility for all that happened to him. I have asked forgiveness for what befell him through my weakness. I now accept any punishment. I ask for it, beg that whatever punishment from man or God waits to be levied come to me, only me.*

*"Now, instead of protecting what was my son and what my son may be, I turn my energies to you, whatever you are. For you who listens to me on the other side of this door. Who spies on me. Who dogs us all. I have petitioned God to*

*forgive you completely, for all you've done and will do, may do, to forgive you for your very nature. I have asked God and will continue to ask God to transform you. To accept responsibility for you. To redeem you without your request or consent."*

*She looks at me directly. That small human face, eyes open and with a strange expression I have not seen before. She speaks again.*

*"God bless you, creature."*

*She cries.*

*She is Anna the house mistress, Anna the tidier. Anna of old.*

*Anna has always prayed, which I was not privy to. It is a fact though I don't know the cause. I will learn to hear prayers.*

*I remember when we made the ink. It was a human day. She knew what I was and what I was not. She gave herself to the lie for the pleasure of the semblance of her son. I helped her make the very medium by which she confesses.*

*I cannot weep. She cries for me.*

*That is Anna. Surprise. Always. For ever.*

# PART IV

# THE WOMEN

**Walking, they have** this sense that someone is behind them, just out of sight. It's neither a frightening nor a comforting feeling. The ice gleams around them, not melting and yet not solid, porous ice. Soft. The earth glows in lieu of moon and sun. The women want the dawn to come. It delays for ever. Their eyes water and their nostrils drip.

When a vehicle stops, the women refuse to get in but request, through Rachel, that the man notify the police of their need for help. When he leaves, they're uncertain he was what he appeared to be. They huddle, and a common story forms, true, and harmful to no one. Though separated from two of their number, and maybe more, at least one more, they feel aligned, as if bound by a piece of starlight. "We have a history," Deborah says. "We are a team."

Rachel lowers the bag from her shoulder, unzips it, and finds her phone. She turns it on, squinching her eyes in hope. "Connected!" She opens the bag further, spreads a few newspapers on the bag itself and snaps a shot with her phone. She opens the camcorder, folds out the viewing screen, hands the camcorder to Deborah. "I'm going to take photos of the screen shots, so click them as I say."

In a few minutes, she says, "Stop," and fidgets with the phone keys. "I'm sending the photos to me," she explains without looking up. "The police will take everything and I have to save our history, you know? Somebody has to save something! We can prove what we claim and we have to do it."

"You're so quick," Deborah says.

"Not always the right way."

A sole police car arrives, but before the women are even in the vehicle, three more pull off the road ahead of them.

The women are taken to the hospital, they are questioned individually, with no hint of suspicion, questioned again by a different officer. Shelley falls asleep in the midst of answering questions, so pale and fragile her officer leaves her alone. In the halls of the hospital, he and other officers confer. The women are of one accord publicly that the assailant was a man. A ghost man. They are all victims, though only one was stabbed. Every police officer in the department must want to join the file of cars out to that old house, investigating. Backing up. This is going to be a case for the records. The women may go home. Melody will be transported to the Mason hospital. Her wounds will heal. Her heart needs further care. She's more than lucky to have survived. The women should stay available. They will surely be called upon to answer more questions.

"Have someone bring you clothing," an officer says. "We have to keep what you were wearing. Or we could send someone for clothing."

"My husband will come after me," Deborah says.

"Mine too," from Rachel. "Will we be able to get our belongings back? I have lots of notes and research material in my bag. One of your guys took it."

"We'll log everything in carefully. What's yours will be returned if it's not evidence or no longer needed. I can't say when."

They wait in their isolated, cold rooms, each dressed in a paper gown, paper underwear, and paper slippers. They seem to have arrived in a different world. In their minds are words and images for their own time, none else, forever shared. A particular demon intimate to them. And a corpse from long ago, a woman who had been lovely and brave and strong. Was she defeated or victorious? They don't know. And one young man. Ghosts—they exist, without doubt.

Finally the two husbands arrive, and the women are charioted toward home. The sun has been up a long time, coasting in its blue sky over the white, icy, thawing land. It has passed the center of day, heading toward afternoon.

# LUKE ESSEX

**Luke, assured that** his fingers are responding as they should, and his injuries will heal, ponders the varied stories circulating. He recalls falling just at the moment he thought the climb hadn't been so bad, that he was short minutes away from reaching level ground, the house, and the ladies. Isn't that the way of the world? Don't get cocky, ever. He recalls, too, rousing at a strange warmth and a soothing tone he couldn't identify, and crying because though he felt safe, he knew he might have broken both arms irreparably. *Let my music not be gone. Let it not!* That had been his prayer. Then had come clatter and yells, and he was gathered up by three or four men onto a stretcher and inserted into an ambulance and closely cared for. He makes no bones about telling the truth when questioned. "Yes, I've heard the place is haunted, but I've been there often and nothing untoward ever happened. There's an old mattress in the basement, tramps and hunters have probably rested there, not all of them good men. I don't know who hurt that woman." Fondness swells in him for someone in a blue dress, and he hastens to say, "I don't believe it was one of the other women. Whatever the women say is likely true."

# HOMEWARD
# DEBORAH

**On the south** side of the highway between Sedalia and Mason is an old, cracked, but erect stone silo. A tree grows from the top and has for years, going through the seasons alone, like a prince or princess, or a remnant of the tower of Babel. Deborah loves the tower and the stories it suggests. "You've seen that tower?" She half turns to address Shelley and hears the murmured, "many times." Were her husband to drive on, and go south toward Holden, they would see the tower of another structure, like a medieval castle surrounded by thousands of trees, so in the verdure of summer the place is hidden. She has intended for years to drive out one day and locate that place. Now, when she's no longer both exhausted and exhilarated, trembling and afire, she is too aware of what peoples the world she lives in but hasn't seen, may never see. How can she tell what she knows? May she teach it? Should she teach it in small secrets that don't alarm the hearer? A leaf, suddenly, brittle and brisk, skips across the windshield, pauses seconds longer than possible, then wheels off into the sky. Deborah snaps around to see Shelley's wide eyes. Innocuous occurrence, and yet. Oh, what they share! Her husband squeezes her knee. Dear man.

# SHELLEY

**Deborah's husband accompanies** Shelley to her apartment and insists on coming in with her. He opens every door and even checks under the beds. When he leaves, she feels all the void in the residence. She has more room. Her skin feels it, a cleanness, like fear has left her and her surroundings. The bedroom dresser still holds the display of remembrances, each item belonging to her mother. A gilt-framed tilting mirror; a heart-shaped box, black, lacquered, the top an unfolding red rose; a porcelain hat-pin vase with three bauble-capped pins; a long, gold-striped cigarette holder; a mesh bag of small stones; a boxed set of cards.

Memories flood her senses, the sharp cry from Melody, the appearance of the thing she stabbed, a man of brown thin air, the shape and heft of the knife in her palm, the plunge of knife into solid flesh. She nearly swoons, grips the dresser. Is she a pawn to every force? Was her own nature what powered the evil? She studies her reflection in the gilded mirror. She closes her eyes and thinks on Melody, the peace of her voice. The comfort in her presence, felt nowhere else. She's not alone. But is she good? With the lights out and a candle on the dresser, she shuffles the cards and opens the mesh bag. She takes one card, face down, from the middle of the deck, and with two fingers pushes a stone, without looking, through the bag's opening. A water stone. She turns over the card. Sun.

# CONNIE

**Connie is so** weary, never as bad as this. What she has learned! She must keep it forefront. Yes. It's true. Scary and true. She wishes she, not Melody, had taken the blows. She was enamored, oh, wasn't she? Of what might be in that house. She wants to hoard the feeling, all of it, even the intensity, the flood of discovery, danger, delight, diminished in the discovery of fear and pain, fear for someone else.

In the front seat, Rachel keeps touching her husband's shoulder or hair, or face. Connie longs to love someone as Rachel does. She wants a future to match this brief past, a worthiness, to keep at least these women in her world. But her future is so slight. The others will move beyond her. They must. It's inevitable.

"Why don't you stay with us tonight?" Rachel says over the seat.

"No. Thanks. I'm all right. Home is best for all of us, don't you think?"

"I don't know. All my definitions got skewed. You're

very welcome to stay. More than tonight. Until you feel ready to be alone."

"I'm ready."

Rachel's husband walks Connie to her door, waits for her to unlock it, and goes in with her.

"I'm all right," she says. "Really. You two go on."

She curls in a chair and leaves the lights off. When she wakes, the moon is up there, ice is everywhere melting and little ripples of water cascade down and over the window. None of it frightens her. She touches the cross she wears.

There is a life after this one, she now knows. Some people are not ready for it, not meant for it. The other women have much to give. They add to the good in this life and they should stay. They'll need help.

# RACHEL

**If there's a** God, he knows what she is. His counterpart knows. A whole universe of life may know what she is. Joe knows, the worst of all to know, Joe. His joy at having her alive shows in every touch, glance, but there, laced underneath, is the restraint of pain, lack of confidence, anger. He embraces her briefly. He kisses her in small pecks. "Tell me everything." When she tries, she sees his mind wander as he stares at her, nodding, a twisted little smile on his lips.

She wants to believe she would turn time back if she could, would never be unfaithful if she had it all to do over. She won't pretend to herself. She's aware of what she is, what a selfish, animal creature she is. She will heal and will offend even her own rules again and again and again. She loves Melody, loves them all, and yet, she isn't deterred from wanting. The desire just shifts, grows. She wants to know every detail behind every door, every act, in every mind. She wants to own that whole damned house and drive everyone away until she has scraped it to the bone. She wants to write about it and tell the world. Yet, the desire to protect is overwhelming. The creature in the passage—woman, ghost, spirit, angel—was fragile. What could happen should she, Rachel, open that world in the wrong way, at the wrong time? Already they had almost killed Melody and might have lost Shelley.

Next to her husband, she makes herself smaller, drawing her legs up and lowering her head to his shoulder. He bends his arm so he can tousle her hair. He blows a kiss to her lips. Smudges on the patio window catch the light in their curves, seem to move, to whorl. Rachel closes her eyes. "Love you, Joe," she whispers. She'll try to be better. Give it her best effort. That's all she can do.

# MELODY

**When her husband** leaves the hospital, reluctantly, Melody stares at the white wall. She remembers Shelley, the blur of her twisting and thrusting, never at Melody. The wildness of it. Melody herself trying to grasp the girl, hold her fast. Failing. One blow after another. Shelley's tortured face looking down at her, blue eyes stricken, weeping, her lips pressed tight in a grimace. The stillness. Weakness. They were not alone—something had them both. She draws away from the memory, thinks on Ben, who is himself a great comfort and hope. She doesn't want to sleep but must. A body must heal. She has to let fear fade. She closes her eyes to help herself. She sees the cemetery walk, the haughty fellow who played ghost. Was ghost. Had he followed her or had she followed him? It didn't matter. There he was. He had always been around. She knew him. The world knew him. And Shelley knew him. They would find ways to deal with him. Her body shivers. She'll check on Shelley later, tonight or tomorrow. Rachel. Connie and Deborah, too, but Shelley first.

# SPRINGTIME

## ANNA

**It is springtime.** I recognize the random blossoms on the grounds of this place. I believe I planted the seeds long ago. The flowers will dry and die when the hot weather comes and be replaced by those intended for full sun. Then the fall blooms. Time flits around, like droplets of memory, bursts of the good and bad.

People came to strip the house of whatever they could find. They didn't meddle long, sensing a darkness that made them cringe from carrying away anything. One of them deliberately set a fire, but it extinguished itself, as if fire has no power here. The caretaker comes and sometimes plays. The music twines among the leaves, through the open windows, cleansing like a blessing. My attic bedroom has no door at all, no cross in any window. No Anna either, though the bed remains. They have taken my bones and John's and have, I pray, interred them as I wished.

I have no true sanctuary now, but this is my place. I

believe I will see my son again, whole. And William. He must be fighting a battle, making choices, leaving memories. He comes this way. He will cross whatever fathoms lie between us and will come heartily home, calling "Anna!" He will grab me up and rub that rough beard against my neck, and I will feel so full of love and life that I will sing all night and day. My waiting is my faith. If that is not to be, I serve my purpose here. I can cross the bridge. I can go down the slight bank and plunge my fingers in the trickle of water and bring up pebbles. I can roam the woods behind the house and I can stand on a high hill above a school. I claim this place for whatever is good.

A vehicle comes from the highway, arrives covered with rust. A woman leaves it far across the yard. It is Connie. Constance. Constance the courageous. She comes toward the house, carries a metal cup, and sips from it. She doesn't see me. She stays there awhile, then suddenly starts for the back steps and I dart inside to meet her in the great room. I am excited and alarmed.

She enters, seems dismayed that everything has changed, has been stripped of its beauty and comfort. She lowers herself down with a groan and sits on the floor.

"I'm really tired," she says. "You understand."

She is speaking to me.

"I'm grateful to you," she says. "We all are. I wish I could see you. Are you here?" She sips from the cup again,

again. "We love you, Anna. You dear woman. I want to join you. I want to do battle. I've been beaten down, but there's a chance for me. I see it. I want to take it, to offer myself up in this fight." She sips again. "Are you here? Please let me see you."

I try. I step forward and hold my arms out. Here! I feel my own ineptitude. I don't have that skill, such a simple thing. Perhaps it must be the two of us and she doesn't have the skill either.

"I am here, Constance."

She waits. Then she takes from her black shirt a photograph and lays it on the floor before her. "Rachel gave this to me. She gave one to each of us." She removes the top from her cup, drinks what remains and replaces the top. She lies partway down, propping her head and shoulders up. She sighs. Her face is terribly lined, etched patchwork. Her lips are parched and cracked. She lies fully prone, on her back. She closes her eyes.

Time passes. I watch her face ease into sleep. The light plays through the windows and across the floor. I hear my son's voice in the sound of birds and breezes. When I look at her again, I realize what she has done, and in my presence. She has learned from me the wrong lesson! She has chosen her death. After all that struggle, she chooses this. She takes my path but for her own reason. Is she mistaken? Is the choice not hers, just the act, not its end?

I try to rouse her. I kiss the worn cheeks, chafe her hands. "Connie! Connie! It's Anna. Wake."

I wonder if guilt will always be my lot, is my lot. I slip my hand inside the curve of hers. If there is a breath, I neither hear it nor feel it. She is peaceful.

He watches. I have no doubt. Does he gloat? Wonder? Outside, the sun streams brighter for seconds, slides through the room. I don't know if Connie will be here with me or not. She may have a place to go and something to enjoy or achieve. I have questions and hope. No power. After a while, I am drawn toward the photograph. A gift. The image is not clear but it is discernible. It is in the passage. I recognize the close, dark walls. A person has been captured. She is a small woman, smaller than I have believed myself to be, and very pale, vapory. Surely that is a kind face, though the eyes are sad. Around the body, which I am afraid is my own, as it is now, is a kind of aura, more than glow, not complete. Whatever I am becoming, I am so very slow.

# AUTHOR'S NOTE

I've written for a long time about the battle between good and evil—the roles we play, the lines we draw, and the resources we have, whether or not we know it. I'm not writing about societal norms or casting blame but following characters as they search for truth and happiness. The women here, strangers to me years ago, are now dear. I'm interested in your thoughts and questions about the work, so please review the book if you have time, and send your queries to my email through rmkinder.net.

R. M. Kinder

# ACKNOWLEDGMENTS

I would like to thank each person who shared with me stories and beliefs about ghosts and the afterlife, but that would be difficult. The conversations occurred over a number of years and with multiple people, even strangers — I might forget someone or inadvertently name a person who preferred anonymity. Some friends and family members warned me about the dangers of research and writing about ghosts. I thank them for their concern, which I share. A few people were invaluable as readers and editors: Holli Burge, Chuck Hoctor, Jim Taylor, Chanda Zimmerman, Audrey Martin, Stephanie Flint, and, as always, my daughter Kristine Martin. A special thanks goes to Ken Baker, who has steadily been my tech support in managing computers, printers, and many near disasters in writing and publishing.

# OTHER BOOKS
# BY R. M. KINDER

Absolute Gentleman

Cat for All Seasons

Common Person & Other Stories

Near-Perfect Gift & Other Stories

Old Time Fiddling: Hal Sappington, Missouri Fiddler

Sweet Angel Band & Other Stories

Universe Playing Strings

**As B.A.L. McMillan**

Strains of Long Ago (novelette)

That Other World (Stories)

Tune of Murder